By Penelope Fitzgerald

The Gate of Angels

PENELOPE FITZGERALD

The GATE *of* ANGELS

NAN A. TALESE

DOUBLEDAY

New York   London   Toronto   Sydney   Auckland

C · 1

PUBLISHED BY DOUBLEDAY

a division of
Bantam Doubleday Dell Publishing Group, Inc.
666 Fifth Avenue, New York, New York 10103

DOUBLEDAY and the portrayal of an anchor
with a dolphin are trademarks of
Doubleday, a division of Bantam Doubleday Dell
Publishing Group, Inc.

Published by arrangement with HarperCollins Publishers, Limited.

Library of Congress Cataloging-in-Publication Data

Fitzgerald, Penelope.
The gate of angels / Penelope Fitzgerald.
p.   cm.
I. Title.
PR6056.I86G3   1992
823'.914—dc20   91-4258
                                              CIP

ISBN 0-385-42150-8

10   9   8   7   6   5   4   3   2   1

First Edition in the United States of America

CONTENTS

Part One

Part Two

Part Three

Part Four

The Gate of Angels

Part One

Chapter One

FRED'S THREE NOTES

How could the wind be so strong, so far inland, that cyclists coming into the town in the late afternoon looked more like sailors in peril? This was on the way into Cambridge, up Mill Road past the cemetery and the workhouse. On the open ground to the left the willow-trees had been blown, driven and cracked until their branches gave way and lay about the drenched grass, jerking convulsively and trailing cataracts of twigs. The cows had gone mad, tossing up the silvery weeping leaves which were suddenly, quite contrary to all their experience, everywhere within reach. Their horns were festooned with willow boughs. Not being able to see properly, they tripped and fell. Two or three of them were wallowing on their backs, idiotically, exhibiting vast pale bellies intended by nature to be always hidden. They were still munching. A scene of disorder, tree-tops on the earth, legs in the air, in a university city devoted to logic and reason.

Fairly was making the best pace he could. He did not much like being overtaken by other bicyclists. No-one likes being overtaken by other bicyclists. The difficult conditions (some were blown over) turned the Mill Road into a display of pride.

The year was 1912 so that Fairly's bicycle, a Royal Sunbeam, must have been thirteen years old. It had Palmer tyres, which left a pattern of long lines like wires, on a wet, glass-clear road. He felt better when he overtook a man who, from the back, might have been someone he knew slightly, and turned out in fact to be someone he knew slightly, a lecturer in the Physiology of the Senses, who called out:

9

'They can't get up again, you know, poor beasts, poor brute beasts!'

He was shouting. It was like sea-bathing. Everyone in turn must swerve to avoid a hat which had blown off and was darting about, crushed and deformed, at random. A whole group went by, then one of them detached himself and was riding alongside.

'Skippey!'

He couldn't hear what Skippey said, so dropped back and came up on the other side, the lee side.

'You were saying?'

'Thought is blood,' Skippey replied.

The first man, the acquaintance, caught up once more. They were three abreast.

His words streamed with the wind.

'I was in error. It's sheep that can't get up, sheep.'

'The relief of it!' Fairly called back. Now that the rain had stopped for a moment the drops blew off the trees as hard as handfuls of gravel.

At Christ's Pieces Fairly turned right, meeting the wind head-on, and made landfall at his own college, St Angelicus.

Angels was, as it is, a very small college. Jokes about the difficulty of finding it, and the troubles the inmates were put to in fitting into it, had been made at any time for the past five hundred years. The twentieth century had opened by increasing these difficulties – for example, in the case of the Fellows' bicycle shed, crouched like a peasant shack on the inner wall, close to the Founder's Entrance. Peasants, however, would have built this, or any other shack, out of the way of the wind and rain, whereas the bicycle shed, on three sides, was open to both. And then, who might have arrived there before you? The college tutor of Angels was, and had been since the Second Boer War, a volunteer with the East Anglian Territorial Bicycle Corps, and, largely for reasons of vanity, rode at all times his specially adapted safety machine with its leather case for signal flags, rifle rest and spare water barrel. It occupied its own space and three-eighths of the next one, so that if you were the last man in, as Fairly appeared to be this evening, there was nothing for it but to manhandle your own bicycle onto a large iron hook fixed by the porter in the upper part of the wall.

Rain streamed down Fairly's face, gathered at the tip of his nose, and fell. The shed was not so much like a shack, perhaps, as like the dodger on a ship's bridge, of which one could only say that it was just about drier inside it than out. One step into the dusk, though, and he was through the Founder's Arch and then into the inner court, with its one great walnut tree. Here, cut off completely, the wind could hardly be felt. Feeling as though he had been stunned, or dreaming, and was still dreaming, he began a short diagonal walk across the grass to get to his own rooms in the north-west corner. From the larger darkness under the trees a patch of darkness detached itself. It was the Master of the College, his gown scarcely adrift in the quiet airs of the Court of Angels.

The Master was blind. Fairly hesitated. After thirteen years the Master might have been expected to know the ins and outs of his little college, and he did know them. Probably he had paused under the walnut tree to sense what the crop was likely to be. It was an old sort, a Cornet du Périgord, which flowered late.

The Master called out, scarcely raising his voice, however. 'This grass is reserved for the Fellows of this college. Should you be walking on this grass?'

'Yes, I should, Master.'

'But who is it?'

'It's Fred Fairly.'

'Fairly, didn't you have an accident? An accident quite recently?'

'Yes, I did.'

'On your bicycle, or off your bicycle?'

'I suppose, both.'

'I hope you weren't unwise enough to go to hospital?'

'I'm all right now, Master.'

'Please take my left arm.'

This had to be done in a particular way, laying two fingers only on the forearm. It was the Master, however, who did the steering, slowly round and once again around the great tree trunk. He said quietly, 'You're very wet, Fairly.'

'Yes, Master, I'm sorry about that.'

'Now, tell me, have you made up your mind on the most important question of all?'

'You're talking about my religious beliefs?'

'Good God, no!'

A rectangle of light opened in a wall and the Senior Tutor came out and took affectionate charge of the Master, who did not need it in the least.

'Senior Tutor, just one or two points. In the first place, Fairly is very wet, for some reason. Where does he keep?'

'I think, in the north-west corner.'

'And then, Senior Tutor, there are kittens somewhere on our premises, very young ones. I heard them distinctly. As with all mammals, their first sounds are angry, the pleading note comes later.'

'Possibly in the kitchens,' the Senior Tutor said. 'I shall speak to the Steward.'

As on Mount Athos, no female animals capable of reproduction were allowed on the college premises, though the starlings couldn't altogether be regulated. There were no women bedmakers or cleaners of any age. These were very ancient regulations. Fairly continued on his diagonal. When he reached the bottom of his staircase he took off his Burberry, hung it on the ancient newel post and gave it one or two sharp blows to shake off the damp. Then he went up to the top floor, where he kept. On the way up he passed Beazley, the gyp. Beazley was short, like all the college servants, who were selected, probably, with this in mind. Fred had an arrangement with this man, which they had arrived at five years earlier when he had been appointed as a Junior Fellow, that

Beazley wasn't to ask whether his fire needed making up, because he was perfectly well able to make it up for himself, that he never wanted to order anything up from the kitchens, and that he didn't want to be told that his messages, brought up from the porter's lodge, were urgent.

'These are urgent, Mr Fairly,' said Beazley, catching up with him and handing him three envelopes, two of them clean and one of them not quite.

There was no gas laid on in the college and Fred turned on the Aladdin lamp, which threw a circle of inner radiance, as calm as it was bright. The fire was banked up like a furnace, dividing the room into areas of dismaying heat and cold. Up here the wind could be heard once again, battering at the panes for admission, while the roof-slates braced themselves against a fall. The college had never been thoroughly heated or dried out since its foundation, but Fred, who had been brought up in a rectory, one of the draughtiest places on earth, saw no reason to complain. He hung up his boots, his socks, his sock-suspenders, his cap, like offerings to the fire-God, on the solid brass fender. They steamed, and his long-jointed feet also steamed. Being too late for dinner in Hall, he took a knife and a cottage loaf out of a cupboard and began to make himself toast. He knew how fortunate he was to have got a Junior Fellowship at Angels.

The first note was from the Master. The writing sloped a good deal downwards, but it was clear enough. 'I have to apologise to you for saying, or implying, just now in the court, something that was not true. I asked you who you were, but I, of course, knew who you were. I know the voices of everyone in the college. I also know their steps, even on the grass – particularly on the grass. Normally you cross the court directly from the SSW to the NNE, but this evening you did not do this. You must have walked a little up the gravel path, and that confused me. My remark, I am afraid, reflected something of my annoyance at that confusion.' The Master was fond of sending these notes in the interest of truth, or rather with the intention of going to bed every night in the knowledge that he had neither said or written anything untruthful which he had not corrected. For the Master, it was a very short note. And Fred had learned to live among these people and indeed (as with the cold in his room) already found it difficult to imagine anything else.

The second note was from Skippey, who must have dropped it in to the lodge on his way back to his own college, Jesus. It read, 'Dear Old Fellow, I don't think you heard me just now on Mill Road. Thorpe has let us down to-night on the Disobligers' Society. He says he is ill. He calls it influenza, and we call it letting us down. It's lucky that you've recovered from your accident, because we want you to speak for us in the debate to-night. We want you to speak against the motion. The motion is "that the soul doesn't exist, has never existed, and that it isn't desirable that it should exist". Charles Reding is going to propose the motion. The point is that he's a theologian, and a pious fellow, and so on, and so of course he'll have to say that there's nothing we can be sure of except the body, and that thought is blood, and so on, and then you, Fred, as a rank unbeliever, will have to stick up for the soul. Afterwards, wine and biscuits. And, Fred – '

Beazley was still hanging about. Fred asked him: 'Did the Master want an answer to his note?'

'He didn't ask for one, Sir.'

I'm a disappointment to Beazley, Fred thought. Steaming socks, making toast, though a lot better, mind you, than he makes it himself – where's the dash, where's the display? Although after the first glance he must have given up all hope of making any substantial amount of money out of looking after me – still, there he is, and I like him, oughtn't I to entertain him a little?

'It seems as if I've got to go out and make a speech, Beazley. It was raining, and I'm just drying out. Do I look untidy?'

'Yes, very untidy, Mr Fairly.'

Beazley went out, quite well pleased, shutting the four-inch oak door, which deadened the sound of his steps as they descended the winding stairs.

Fred looked at his watch. It was a silver watch, belonging to his father, given to him when he took up his appointment, and yet not quite given to him either, since when he went back on vacations his father tended to borrow it back. It came to him that he didn't at all want to go out again to-night, that he had a letter of his own to write which must go off – must – but on the other hand he ought not to disoblige the Disobligers' Society. This was because he had once done Skippey a good turn, something to do with money, a temporary loan, and you are always under an obligation to anyone you've helped once. But his mind had not warmed up at the same rate as his body, and he was not able to think, still less to put in order, what he could possibly say in defence of the soul.

The third note, in the envelope that was not so clean, consisted of a couple of pages torn out of a note-book. It was from an acquaintance. Fred couldn't remember where he had first met Holcombe, or why, having met him but not ever much wanting to see him again, they now considered themselves acquaintances. It was on a subject they had been talking about a couple of days ago. Holcombe must have thought of something else he wanted to say, gone to the lodge, found that Fred had signed out, and immediately started writing, since it would have been as dangerous for him not to express himself as to block his digestive system.

' . . . Long tramps, Fairly, over our beloved Fenland, speaking together of intellectual problems and those only, descending at last after say fifteen miles for whisky and a warm at some friendly Cambridge hearth! That is a man's recreation. Now, if one were to marry – well, look at it in this way – a wife has a legal right to be in the same house and even the same room as oneself! From the point of view of the temptations of the flesh that may be convenient enough, but what if she were to want to *talk*? Your own position is so much simpler. You don't have to make up your mind. At the age of twenty-five years, it is made up for you. If you stay at St Angelicus you can't marry. If you leave, you may get another appointment, but not, you can be pretty certain, another Junior Fellowship. You are choiceless. In fact, you must be careful that your powers of choice don't fall into disuse. I think of rust, I think of springs becoming weaker. You may find you can't remember how to choose at all. And yet the prospect of an alternative is absolutely necessary to human will and human action. Still, let us be honest, there seems no point, as far as I can see, in your ever getting to know any young women at all – '

At this point Holcombe had run out of space. When Fred next met him, he would start straight away from where his letter had broken off, as though between words spoken and words written there was no dividing line.

Out of a carved oak locker on the opposite side of the fire from the coal-scuttle, but distinct from the bread-cupboard (and breathing out a different smell of mould when opened), Fred took a few sheets of the college paper. He shook his fountain pen to see how much ink was left in it, and wrote: 'Dear Miss Saunders'.

Chapter Two

A FEW WORDS ABOUT
ST ANGELICUS

St Angelicus had two great distinctions. One it shared with St Andrew's University. That was that it had no real existence at all, because its foundation had been confirmed by a pope, Benedict XIII, who after many years of ferocious argument had been declared not to be the Pope at all. Two years after he had been legally elected in 1394 he was told that he was dethroned. By every law of God and man, however, no-one on earth had the right to do this. Kings and emperors can be dislodged, but not legally elected Popes. Benedict, too, was an Aragonese, and one of the most obstinate of an obstinate nation. In 1415 he retreated to a castle built on a jagged rock 64 metres high and linked to the mainland of Castellon by a strip of sand, covered at high tide by the sea. Here, in Peñiscola, he continued to hold audience in the vast halls, furnished with books and the rags of tapestries which he had brought with him. No matter, he was now ninety years old, and must die soon. He did not die, and refused to give way an inch. To settle everyone's conscience, it was agreed by the Kings of Europe to arrange for him to be poisoned. Benedict had always lived temperately and had only one weakness left, a fondness for quince preserves, which were made for him by the nuns in a convent on the mainland. After enquiry, a Benedictine was found who was an expert at introducing poison into sweets. An attendant was bribed to take these sweets to the Pope's study. But the old man vomited so hideously that his stomach was cleared. The attendant was arrested, the Benedictine was found guilty and burned alive, and the Pope died five years later, with dignity. He was buried in his home town of Ilueca. During the war of the Spanish succession his body was dug up by French soldiers on the rampage, who cut off the head and threw it away. Rescued from a ditch by an honest labourer, it was preserved as an object of veneration. The Senior Tutor of Angels had in fact made the journey to Aragon to see it, together with Dr Matthews, the Provost of James's, a very well-known antiquarian. A silver reliquary had been opened for them by special arrangement, and they had been allowed a sight of Benedict XIII's skull. Both of them had noticed that the right eye was still visible, hanging at the back of the socket in the form of a kind of dark jelly.

'It was a recognisably human glance, in my opinion,' the Provost had said. 'There seemed a spark. Yes, some kind of communication. If we could have seen the whole skeleton, I fancy it would have had its hand over its heart.' The Chaplain of Angels said later that it had been a mistake for the Senior Tutor to go out to Spain with the Provost, who wrote ghost stories in his spare time, and read them aloud, and who was nothing but an old woman when it came to bones and graveyards. 'And what the two of them must have suffered! You know that in Spain they put pieces of potato in the omelettes. And then, to go on mule-back!'

'I think they took a local train from Zaragoza,' someone corrected him.

'A Spanish train! Worse, much worse,' said the Chaplain.

The second distinction of Angels was its size. It was the smallest college in Cambridge, and had never shown any signs of wanting to extend or expand in any direction. It had been built, at the beginning of the fifteenth century, on a plan as unlike a monastery as possible. Although everything was in miniature, it resembled a fortress, a toy fortress, but a toy of enormous strength, with walls $3\frac{1}{2}$ feet thick, built without rubble. There were no cloisters, no infirmary, no hospice, no welcome (to be honest), to those, strangers or not, arriving from outside, no house apart for the Master, who crowded in on an upper floor along with the Fellows, an arrangement which had caused him to be known in the old days as Master Higgledy-Piggledy. As time went by, more openings in the roof were grudgingly allowed for chimneys, and fireplaces were built in the rooms, and one cold water tap on each landing. As to the students, in 1415 none of the colleges had anywhere for them to sleep, and St Angelicus, in 1912, still hadn't. There were no hostels for them either. They had to find their own lodgings, and six o'clock in the evening took the last of them away, like roosting birds, their chatter fading into the distance, after which they were forgotten till the next morning. There was no room in the court for their bicycles, which had to remain stacked outside the Great Gate. Over the gate the heraldic arms, weathered almost flat with the wall, showed two angels asleep, waiting for the Day of Judgement when Benedict XIII will be shown at last to be indisputably right, and all the proceedings of the Catholic Church since 1396 will be annihilated and trodden into the dust, for all of them have been made on false authority. The motto, *Estoy in mis trece*, not altogether suitable for a place of learning, was one of Benedict's few recorded remarks. It is translated as 'I have not changed my mind', but 'nothing doing' might be nearer.

The college, then, had learned the art of living in a small space. There were the cellars, of course, and these extended beyond the college buildings themselves, some way underneath Butts Green. 1911 had been a good year for hock and champagne, and Angels had laid in considerable supplies, and were debating whether to burrow even further and to construct another vault. But, above ground, there were only the Master, the college servants and six Fellows. In other colleges the Fellows for the past thirty years had been allowed to marry and live out, but in the statutes of St Angelicus this was forbidden. The number of problems which, in consequence, did not need discussing resulted in a great saving of time, but labour, too, had to be saved. The Junior Fellowship which Fred had been granted meant combining the jobs of assistant organist, assistant librarian, deputy steward, and assistant deputy treasurer. The words assistant, deputy, and so forth didn't mean that there was necessarily anyone above him to do the work, only that he must do it without being paid.

Chapter Three

HOW FRED GOT THIS JOB IN
THE FIRST PLACE

Fred had taken the science tripos, and at a gathering for those who had been awarded a First Class degree he had met Professor Flowerdew. There had been music and refreshments in the open air, ruined by a downpour, as often happens in Cambridge, where the rainfall is believed to be low and risks are taken again and again. Everyone had taken refuge in the Cavendish, where Professor Flowerdew, who did not like parties (still less when they were called gatherings) had been all the time. He was just retreating from the physics laboratory, and with one melancholy sideways movement of his head he invited Fred upstairs to his office. This (like most of the rooms, after all) was dark, and reached by a dingy corridor. The walls were covered with photographs, and more photographs were pinned onto the desks. Fred sniffed the air. It was his ambition to have, one of these days, an office in the Cavendish.

Flowerdew sat down at the desk, leaving the stool near the microscope, and said to Fred, 'What do you know about me?'

'I've only just finished my first degree,' Fred replied. 'Truly, I don't know anything.'

'Well, I know something about you. Yes, something. I know you're a bright fellow. I know you come from a rectory family. They say that at the Cavendish we have to make do with apparatus knocked up out of cardboard and string. But if you come from a rectory you'll be used to economies.'

'It's a great thing you've even heard of me at all,' said Fred.

21

'And what next?'

'I had thought of asking Professor Wilson whether I could work with him. I mean in some capacity. I could help with the photographic plates, perhaps. He was my tutor for advanced practical physics.'

'C.T.R. Wilson. A very good, very patient Scotsman. Could you read what he wrote on the blackboard?'

'Usually not. He used to write it with one hand and wipe it off at the same time with the other. But if I had the chance to study his methods – '

'You want to assist him with the construction of his third cloud chamber. You want to photograph the alleged tracks of ionising particles.'

Fred turned red. 'These are wonderful years in Cambridge.'

'You are attracted towards atomic research?'

'I've seen Ernest Rutherford walking into the Cavendish,' Fred cried. 'I heard his lectures. It all hangs together. If it works it must be true.'

'Well, well,' said Professor Flowerdew. 'I expect it will hang together for a considerable time, perhaps sixty or seventy years. The belief that Nature, or an invisible god, created the world and assigned everything for a purpose, lasted very much longer than that and worked reasonably well. But we've given all that up, because we've got no evidence that God or Nature exists.'

'None at all,' said Fred. 'That has to be left to faith. After all, you can only reason from what you can observe.'

'Quite so,' said Professor Flowerdew. 'But atoms are unobservables.' He pointed to one of the photographs on the wall.

'Who is that?' he asked.

Fred floundered, looking at the bearded, enigmatic faces, one of which had been circled in red ink. There were distant men in frock coats and top-hats, standing outside a building he did not recognise.

'That is Ernst Mach, a photograph taken in Vienna on the occasion of his retirement from the University Chair of physics. I used to be in correspondence with him, now I no longer am. It was from his lectures and his *Science of Mechanics* that I came to understand the folly of basing any kind of scientific research on unobservables. Mach, don't forget, is a very deeply respected physicist. He has established, among many other things, the relationship between the speed of objects and the local speed of sound. But in respect of the atom, Mach said to the world, don't commit yourself to it! An atom is not a reality, it is just a provisional idea, so how can we say that it is situated in space? We ought to feel suspicious of it when we find that it has been given characteristics which absolutely contradict those which have been observed in any other body. There is a continuity of scientific thought, you know. The continuity is now being thrown out of the window. Let us hope we shall remember where it is when, at long last, we find that we can't do without it.'

He looked compassionately at Fred. 'You're hungry. But it's of no use going down now, the Science Faculty will have eaten everything. The organic chemists will have cleared the sandwiches. Let me tell you what is going to happen, over the coming centuries, to atomic research.

'There will be many apparent results, some useful, some spectacular, some, very possibly, unpleasant. But since the whole basis of the present research is unsound, cracks will appear in the structure one by one. The physicists will begin by constructing models of the atom, in fact there are some very nice ones in the Cavendish at the moment. Then they'll find that the models won't do, because they would only work if atoms really existed, so they'll replace them by mathematical terms which can be stretched to fit. As a result, they'll find that since they're dealing with what they can't observe, they can't measure it, and so we shall hear that all that can be said is that the position is probably this and the energy is probably that. The energy will be beyond their comprehension, so they'll be driven to the theory that it comes and goes more or less at random. Now their hypotheses will be at the beginning of collapse and they will have to pull out more and more bright notions to paper over the cracks and to cram into unsightly corners. There will be elementary particles which are too strange to have anything but curious names, and anti-matter which ought to be there, but isn't. By the end of the century they will have to admit that the laws they are supposed to have discovered seem to act in a profoundly disorderly way. What is a disorderly law, Fairly?'

'It sounds like chaos,' said Fred.

'The chaos will be in their minds only. It, too, will not be observable.'

'What do you think is to be done?'

'Admit the wrong direction, and go back to what can be known through the senses. If they don't depend on true evidence, scientists are no better than gossips.'

Professor Flowerdew had, he said, been fortunate. The university during the last ten years or so had been surprisingly ready to create, – by Grace, to use their own terms – posts, and even professorships, which would last only for as long as was thought necessary. There were, for instance, travelling bachelorships 'for the encouragement of investigation into foreign countries', established by the Special Board for Military Studies – scholarships in other words for spies. As a kind of counterweight some of the appointments had no apparent practical use whatsoever. Herbert Flowerdew had been offered a temporary Professorship in Observable Experimental Physics.

Fred was shocked by the word 'fortunate'. He felt that luck and chance should have no place in science, and above all at the Cavendish.

'The Cavendish is becoming very crowded,' said Flowerdew. 'There is a pot-house atmosphere. I have arranged to have a small laboratory of my own in the Department of Mechanical Philosophy.' His own experiments were in the principles of equivalence and reciprocity. He couldn't, then, be altogether cracked.

But was it, Fred broke out in distress, that he had no interest in the work of Wilson, and Rutherford, and Planck, and Niels Bohr, whose almost inaudible lectures Fred had also heard that year?

'Not at all. I follow all that they printed with great interest, both through the German and the English journals. I am impressed with their results. I admire their great talents. But when I think of their future I hear the sadness of old men and those whom the gods have deserted.'

Flowerdew needed an assistant at £100 a year, which he would pay himself, to instruct his students in physics and take them off his hands generally. He could guarantee this assistant, too, a Junior Fellowship at St Angelicus. There was a vacancy in the college, not through death, but through a lecturer in Propellant Explosives being unexpectedly recalled to Germany. In explaining this Flowerdew made it quite clear that the Junior Fellow would also have to lend a hand with the library, the catering and the accounts, act as assistant organist, and keep the collection of fifteenth-century musical instruments in repair and, as far as possible, tuned. Here Fred jibbed.

'I can't do that. All I could ever do was to help out at home with the hymns. I've never even seen a fifteenth-century instrument.'

'Let us forget them for the moment. Don't answer me now. Think it over.'

By 'don't answer me now' Flowerdew had meant, 'don't accept straight away because you're a scholarship boy from a rectory with nothing to live on.' Fred was struck by this, and by other things which the Professor was not doing. He was not, like the great ones of Cambridge, keeping a princely look-out for young followers. He wasn't asking Fred to agree with him, either, about the unsoundness of atomic physics; not that. Clearly he was a lonely man, but he had made nothing of his loneliness, either. And there was a lack, not of self-confidence, but of self-assurance, in all this, that Fred liked. He was not vain himself, and only the humble can value humility. It appealed to him, too, that Flowerdew stood as one against many, not because he knew too little, but because he understood too much. 'Stood' was not the right word, though. He was no more likely to make a stand than Fred's own father, gazing out of the window at the Rectory.

Without seeing Flowerdew again, Fred went home to the Rectory, where he was asked by the neighbours (called in to celebrate his First Class in physics) what he expected to do next, and, by the Rural Dean, whether he was going to blow them all up. Then Fred went with two of his friends for a walking holiday in Austria. For the first time in his life he felt he had no obligation to anyone. They went to the Salzburg Alps. At Bruckmann's Hotel, by candlelight, the two wait-resses and the daughter of the house appeared at the door of the three-bed commercial travellers' room which they had taken for cheapness' sake. Fred was the only one not asleep. The situation struck him as like a folk tale. He woke his two friends, and went down with the daughter, who had the keys, to fetch two bottles of wine from the dining-room. More she dare not take. When they got back upstairs the others were all sitting stiffly on the edge of the beds, not undressed, not even speaking, as though waiting for permission to begin. Fred found it hard not to laugh, then they all laughed. The wine was Grüner Weltliner, tasting violently of pepper. They blew out the candles and opened the shutters, to let the stars shine in. The room smelled of the just extinguished candlewicks, of the peppery wine, of strong young women's flesh and of starch, because the maids had been doing the ironing.

Next morning they went on and up the mountain to the haymeadows, past the first rocky slopes where the wild raspberries were almost over, through ice-cold shadow into the sunlight of the upper slopes and almost to the edge of the glacier. They sat down, and the elder of Fred's two friends, who was a chemical engineer, told them that he was going back to Bruckmann's, as he had fallen in love with one of the waitresses. They had their valises with them. He picked up his, took his stick and walked away down the path, the stones slipping away beneath his boots. The remaining friend said that he was doing all he could to get to Manchester, in the hope of training with Rutherford. Fred must come too, everything of importance was happening in Manchester.

'No, I'm going back to Cambridge. Herbert Flowerdew has offered me a post as his assistant.'

The friend burst into tears. He had been working far too hard and for too long. He regarded Fred as lost. 'You never said anything about this before.'

'I've only just decided to accept.'

'Come to Manchester.'

'I've decided to accept.'

Chapter Four

DINNER AT ST ANGELICUS

When James I said that a man should pray at King's, dine at Trinity, and study at Jesus, he added (on one occasion at least) 'and he should sleep in peace at Angels'. This did not mean that you got a poor dinner at St Angelicus – quite the contrary, – only that room could hardly have been found at the table for the King's bodyguard and followers. Adapting to the allotted space was, and continued to be, a matter of practice. At other colleges, sherry was served in the combination room, dinner in Hall, brandy in some other sanctuary. At Angels there was the Hall only. Gas-lighting had never been introduced, or even suggested. The candles burned in ancient holders which grasped them in twisted silver rings that held them absolutely straight. Yet that was hardly necessary, since Angels was the only Hall in Cambridge which was not a meeting place of cold draughts. The college silver, acquired at intervals over four hundred years, was largely Spanish, mostly bought from needy church treasuries. Possibly not all of it had been designed as tableware. There were silver objects whose use was not known – a set of instruments, for example, which appeared to be tooth-pullers, and another like a horse comb. Of what use could this have been in the *iglesia mayor* of Morella? However, they glittered on the table every night, and were put back into drawers in the silver pantry. There was an endearing carelessness about it all. Round the table (not the High Table, because there was only one), the company, sitting close together, looked like friendly conspirators. They drank manzanilla imported for them from San-

lúcar, until the butler came in. 'The Master is on his way.'
Everyone got to their feet. With his chair drawn back for him
to exactly the right distance, the Master needed no guidance,
and none was offered. The Chaplain pronounced a grace
which was used on domestic occasions by Benedict XIII
himself, followed by the menacing Spanish words – *El Juicio
Final descubrirá las secretas de la Historia.* All the chairs
trundled back, and those who had dropped their napkins
disappeared for a moment, recovering them. The manzanilla
continued with the soup, and changed to champagne for the
fish course only. After that it was claret at St Angelicus. At the
end the guests were always offered preserved fruits, of the kind
which failed to poison their Founder.

Only one guest could be invited at a time, and the honour
went strictly in turns. One who came quite often, since several
of the Fellows were fond of inviting him, was Dr Matthews,
the Provost of James's. He was a mediævalist and
palaeographer, who, as a form of relaxation, wrote ghost
stories. If he had written one recently, he brought it with him
in an envelope and read it aloud after dinner. He did not care
to be asked to do this. But the shape of the envelope, if he had
it with him, was clearly visible in his overcoat pocket. His host
for the evening would speak unobtrusively to the butler.
'Foley, I want to know whether Dr Matthews brought a large
envelope with him.' Foley was quite up to this. 'He didn't, sir,
not tonight, sir.' Then there would be no reading, but
perhaps music. In some colleges – King's, for example – they
talked all evening, but then King's was full of historians and
philosophers, who had no need to relax. What else did they
ever do? But the Fellows of Angels, by statute, were all
scientists, or mathematicians.

Fred's own unhappy moments in college were connected
with the cittern, the vielle, the zinke and so forth, which he
wasn't persuaded were ever meant, even if tuned, to be played
together. It was only the knowledge that the blind Master
delighted in them that kept him tinkering away at them. He

was more at home with the positive organ, with a keyboard of twenty-two long and thirteen short keys, which was installed in a shadowy corner of the little chapel. Fortunately, the bellows were in poor condition, and it could not be pumped. But Dr Matthews, in any case, was not particularly fond of music. In fact, he was tone-deaf, preferring to look at old manuscripts and to examine ancient inscriptions. He had a running joke, for example, with the Master about the strangely tall and narrow gate, as old as the college itself, in the south-west wall. 'The only opening, dear Master, – apart from your front entrance – and quite inexplicable, since the only thought in the mind of the builders seems to have been to keep visitors out.' There was no inscription on the gate, and no entry, in the records of the college expenses, for installing it. On the other hand it was noted in the annals that it had twice been found standing open, once on the 21st of May 1423, the night of Pope Benedict's death, and once in 1869, when the first women's college, though not, of course, officially part of the University, was permitted to open. 'There was no mention, on either occasion, of who opened your gate,' said Dr Matthews, 'nor of who shut it again.'

'No-one, not even the Master, has any authority to do either,' said the Treasurer.

'But if anyone had, or even if they had not, and if it were to stand open, who or what do you imagine might come in?'

'I should not like to think about that,' said the Master.

Dr Matthews turned to another subject – the manuscripts in the Angels' library. Earlier on he had been looking, he said, at a mediæval Book of Hours, fantastically illuminated by Jean Pucelle. Wherever there was a space between the lines on the page it would be filled with a long, lean, sinuous tail, belonging to a rat, a monster, or a devil. The devil's tails were frequently curled, like a noose, round the neck of unfortunate men. 'Ready, I fancy, to carry them off,' said Dr Matthews, with his delightful smile. He pointed out that most of these victims were alchemists or heretical arithmeticians, and that in the fourteenth and fifteenth centuries all his kind hosts, at present sitting round the table, might well have been condemned to hell.

The Fellows of St Angelicus listened to Dr Matthews with amusement. He was a great scholar, but his lifework seemed to them musty. Dr Matthews, for his part, was amused by the Angels. Science, he thought, was leading them nowhere, and quite conceivably backwards.

Chapter Five

AT THE RECTORY

At the end of his first year as a Junior Fellow, Fred thought it only right to tell his father that he was no longer a Christian, but in such a way as to distress him as little as possible. All this sounded more like 1857 than 1907. He had heard family stories, distant echoes or reminiscences of giant battles from what seemed heroic days. Two of his uncles had quarrelled over Strauss's *Leben Jesu* and struck each other and one of them had caught his head on the edge of the fender and broken his skull. The other one, Uncle Philip, had been known for the rest of his life, though never in the family, as Slayer Fairly. In his mother's family there were some who hadn't spoken to each other for many years, and there were women, once young, who had broken off their engagements because their betrothed had ceased to believe and who had bleached and withered into spectres of themselves behind church missionary society typewriters and the stalls of jumble sales. Fred, who was kind-hearted towards the past as well as the present, felt that he ought not to fall short, in the new century, of what had cost so dear. He ought to go home and explain to his father in person, even giving his reasons, as sons had once done on this subject where reason, not much to its credit, is powerless. So much was only decent politeness. But his father was certain to be deeply distressed. The time of day for discussing this, long enough to give pain and, if possible, to lessen it to some extent, was between five and six o'clock, when his father sat patiently in his study ready to give advice to his parishioners, who, however, always chose some other time to come. The study windows faced the front lawn, and in summer Fred and his two sisters had not been supposed to cross it, between five and six, so as not to disturb the pastoral hour. Fred, Hester and Julia did, of course, cross it, as Apaches, flat on their stomachs, close to the bitter-smelling roots of the laurel hedge where the cat left the remains of her mice. Looking, in those days, up the slight incline of the lawn Fred used to see his father at his desk, determinedly wide awake, his head a little on one side, presumably to show that he was willing and ready to listen, staring out into the late afternoon.

The best thing would be to explain at once that as from the beginning of that summer he was an unbeliever, but his unbelief was conditional. He had no acceptable evidence that Christianity was true, but he didn't think it impossible that at some point he might be given a satisfactory reason to believe in it. And then you'd give it another chance, his father was likely to answer. – That's very handsome of you, Freddie. What would you consider a satisfactory answer? – Well, Father, put it another way. I want to know the truth about the way things are. I can't take them on trust, that would be the waste of the education you've given me and such brains as I've got. – Now – the 'now' didn't sound quite as Fred wanted it, but no matter – the only evidence we can get is from our own senses and from the senses of other people who have gone before us, and can communicate what they found out through writing. – Like the Gospel writers, his father would say – even if they were only a committee. Do you consider they were wasting their time? Yours too, of course. – Do what he could, Fred always found that when he talked to his father, who was not at all deaf, he raised his voice slightly, while his father countered by talking even more quietly than usual. – However, Father, he would go on. You stay close to experience, you see the resemblances between things and the continuity of one idea from another, and gradually, through many lifetimes, everything becomes explained. As soon as something's completely described, it's explained – like the anatomy of the human body, for instance. There's no more to say about that, it can be described, therefore there's no mystery in it, it's ordinary. Well, the time will come when we shall see everything that once seemed extraordinary as ordinary. – Would you prefer that? his father would ask doubtfully. Would you, Freddie?

All this time Fred saw himself walking up and down the study, while his father sat there with his green spectacle-case in his hand, but this walking up and down might suggest that he wasn't sure of himself, so he sat himself down, in his imagination, in one of the not too comfortable chairs. His father, meanwhile, would in all probability go back to his question, the one that had not been answered. – You haven't told me yet, Freddie, what you would consider a satisfactory reason for believing that Christ rose from the dead? – Fred saw himself here listening to his father's voice, in order to judge how much his feelings had been hurt. The next thing would be a knock on the door, as his mother was unable to leave anyone alone in the study for more than twenty minutes without asking them whether they would like to take a little some-thing, perhaps barley water. The barley water was kept on the slate window-sill of the larder, in a jug covered with muslin weighed down at the edge by blue beads.

At this point he saw that he would have to start the discussion at a different point altogether. It was absurd for him to sound as if he was lecturing his father. What he really wanted to explain, stage by stage, was how the crawler across lawns and reliable Sunday choirboy who had sung, with all his heart's conviction,

> Teach me to live that I may dread
> The grave as little as my bed

had become what he now was, a man with a mind cleared and perpetually being recleared (because there was a constant need for that) of any idea that could not be tested through physical experience. There were no illusions left there now. The air was pure. But it had happened gradually, and although Fred wasn't much given to talking about himself he would have, on this occasion, to account for himself gradually. He would have to describe for his father, step by step, how he had expelled the comforting unseen presences which, in childhood, had spoken to him and said: Give me your hand. What is completely described, however, he kept reminding himself, is completely explained.

He got up early, biked to the station, left his bike there and took the train to Blow Halt, changing at Bishop's Leaze. The whole village, from wall to wall of its cottage gardens, blazed with flowers, early phlox and bean-flowers contending with raucous gusts of scent, early roses red and white, pot marigolds, feverfew which was grown here as a garden plant, ferocious poppies and cornflowers, peonies, sweet williams still in flower, herb of grace, Russell lupins, pinks. Nature here was certainly not at her most natural. Most of the cottagers knew where to ask for field manure, the postman and the policeman, seen working every evening in their gardens in their shirtsleeves, had their own arrangements for getting it, and every household emptied its tea-leaves three times a day on the soil, and by night the contents of the earth closets. There was nowhere in Blow to buy vegetables and it never occurred to anyone to buy any. The station grew roses and beans, and large marrows striped like a tom-cat. Even the weeds were not more luxurious than what was grown deliberately.

At Blow Halt he was Mr Fred and had once been Master Freddie, though, once again, he couldn't remember when the change took place. This was Ellsworthy, the station master, who had become Old Ellsworthy.

'We stopped for five minutes outside Bishop's Leaze,' said Fred, 'why was that, do you think?'

'I don't know,' said Ellsworthy. 'I shall have to make enquiries about that.'

'Couldn't you telephone down the line?'

'I *could*.'

Ellsworthy walked with him to the barrier, watched by the very young porter who was lining up the milk-churns. A certain amount of milk always got spilled on the platform, giving it a faint smell of a nursery sink, drowned at the moment by the bean-flowers and the meadowsweet.

'How am I going to find them at the Rectory, Ellsworthy?'

'Why do you ask me, Mr Fred?' Fred didn't know, he hadn't meant any harm. He knew very well, however, that the country is not a place of peace, and that it was difficult to tell what might give or have given offence, which made it a good preparation for life at a university. In this instance, it had probably been a mistake to mention the unscheduled stop at Bishop's Leaze. 'Why do you ask me about the Rector?' repeated Ellsworthy, with controlled fury. 'You can't accuse me of being a church-goer.'

'I don't accuse you of anything,' said Fred. Ellsworthy relented a little, and asked him how things were in London. Fred explained that he was still at Cambridge, but sometimes it was handier to go up to London King's Cross and make the exchange there.

'Yes, London's useful for that,' said Ellsworthy. In the field next to the station fence an old horse, once grey, now white, moved a few sedate steps away. This was a token retreat only, it was many years since the train's approach had given warning that it might be required to pull the station fly. The fly mouldered away now, its shafts pointing upwards, in the corner shed. On the horse's hollow back, as it came to a standstill, the elder flowers fell gently.

There was a short cut through a wicket gate across the field to the Rectory, but Fred could see that it was jammed fast with nettles and trails of blackberry. He could also sense that Ellsworthy was waiting until he pushed the gate to tell him that it was stuck and that he'd do best to go round by the road.

'I'll go round by the road,' he said.

'I can remember when you'd have jumped that. You were quite agile as a boy. You wouldn't have made anything of it.'

Fred began to walk up the road, swinging his bag in his hand: Church Road. The church and Rectory were once imposingly, now unacceptably, at the top of a steep slope. It took it out of you getting up there, if you wanted the Rector to sign a certificate. Elms sheltered the field, young elders and hazels filled the drainage ditches. All that ought to be cleared away before winter, if someone could be found to do it. The Herefords chewed, every jaw moving anti-clockwise, as a tendril grows. Round them the grass stood unmoving, hazed over with a shimmering reddish tinge, ready for hay. The bushes, too, were motionless, but from the crowded stalks and the dense hedges there came a perpetual furtive humming, whining and rustling which suggested an alarming amount of activity out of sight. Twigs snapped and dropped from above, sticky threads drifted across from nowhere, there seemed to be something like an assassination, on a small scale, taking place in the tranquil heart of summer. Fred pounded steadily up the road, which had never been tarmacked and was deeply rutted with cart-tracks which the sun had dried to powder.

Having arrived at a course of action, you should go over it in your mind only once and then prevent yourself from thinking about it until the moment comes. Fred had already decided to speak separately to his mother and to his sisters, Hester aged twenty (he was sure about that) and Julia, who must be sixteen, as she seemed to have stopped learning anything. Separately, because they were scarcely ever in the same room or of the same opinion. There was a kind of agreement to disagree which, however, produced a perfectly orderly life, from day to day, in the Fairly household.

The Rectory had been built in 1830 with a solid dignity which, for the last twenty years or so, had been letting in the water everywhere. The front gate, however, was quite new, and had been designed by the Christian Arts and Crafts Guild of Coventry. It was made of pickled oak, carved and inlaid with copper medallions and what looked like small glazed saucers. The raised lettering read The Rectory, and below that, Welcome, Enter, Have no Fear, Simplicity and Quiet Dwell Here. These two lines, perhaps fortunately, were in a decorative celtic alphabet which was almost impossible to read. The gate had been a gift to the Rector's predecessor who had been artistic, and it was almost the only part of the house in perfect working order.

Rain-faded notices were pinned to the gate concerning a flower show in aid of the Zenana Mission and the Men's Bible Hour, which was cancelled. Fred, who had grasped the curiously-wrought bronze handle, let the latch drop and went round to the back. This was the domain of gooseberry bushes, on which the white washing was spread out to dry, and the rhubarb which had shot up its coarse green leaves high above the old zinc bucket which was supposed to blanch it. Under the lean-to stood a vast mangle, the remains of a bee-hive, a lawn-tennis court marker, which was unlikely ever to mark again, two broken hymn-boards and an ancient bier which had been banished by the parochial church council from the vestry. Why were all these things not got rid of? Fred reproached himself. Nothing was got rid of at the Rectory. It was left to decay at its own pace. While nature rioted outside with her greenstuff, it was perpetual autumn there.

A dog barked inside the house. There were two dogs, Sandford and Merton. Sandford, who would have known Fred's footstep even if he had been returning from the dead, ran out, still barking. Two or three rooks sailed up from the elms, made a circuit through the blue air and sank back into the rookery. They, too, knew Sandford's bark. After him out came Julia, wildly energetic, pigtailed and damp with heat. Her embrace, dear Julia, was more like a collision.

'Freddy, Freddy, Freddy!'

'Julia.'

'Why didn't you telegraph? I knew they were all cold hearts in Cambridge.'

'I wrote,' said Fred, half suffocated. 'I wrote a letter to Father. Here I am like Odysseus, with only an old dog to recognise me.'

'We're in the morning room,' shouted Julia, dragging him through a glassed-in passage, a kind of conservatory which conserved nothing. Sandford was not allowed further than this, and retreated in misery to a soap-box where Merton was already curled up, comatose. Julia led the way into the empty kitchen. The clock ticked, the oven was cold.

'Is there anything to eat?' Fred asked.

'There's some rook pie and sago pudding left over for to-night. They're very nasty, but you remember that we're poor and have to eat nasty things.'

'Where's Mrs Burden?'

'She's in the morning room. We're all in the morning room.'

'It's the afternoon, Julia.'

'We started at six o'clock. You'll see how it is, we can't move everything now.'

They were all of them round the table, his mother, Hester, Mrs Burden who came up from the village to cook and do the rough. All three of them were sewing, Mrs Burden at the treadle sewing machine. There were yards of material everywhere, violet, green, and white, the white looking as if they'd been cutting up pillow-cases. All of them got up. Drapery fluttered from their laps. Julia went down on hands and knees on a length of purple cotton.

'Here you are, purple for justice.'

'My dear Freddy!' said Mrs Fairly. 'What an unexpected pleasure.'

Hester, not quite as cool as usual, said, 'I expect you can see what we're doing. These are the WSPU colours. We're making banners for the Birmingham march. They say they can't have too many.'

'But Mother, you're not interested in Women's Suffrage,' said Fred. 'I've talked to you about it often.'

'She is now, we all are,' said Julia. 'You can't have made the slightest impression on her. Heaven help the people who have to go to your lectures.'

'It's all changed, Freddy,' said Hester. 'It's different now. Nobody laughs now. We saw the photograph of the hunger-strikers in the Daily Mail.'

'You don't read the Daily Mail.'

'I do,' said Mrs Burden.

'Mrs Burden showed it to us in the first place,' said Mrs Fairly. 'Poor young woman, with her eyes shut and her mouth open. She was very far gone.'

'Did she die?'

'We can't find out,' said Hester.

Fred could see that there were letters cut out of the material, question-marks also.

'People don't understand "suffrage",' Hester went on. 'They say "if the women want to suffer, let them get on with it." We're just doing the letters for the one question: "Will you give votes to women?" They're going to confront Asquith with that: "Will you give votes to women?"'

Mrs Burden, who had favoured Fred outrageously as a small boy, nodded and started up the treadle machine. It oughtn't to be making a noise like that, he thought, the spindle must be catching. He'd have to see if he could put it right later. But if he did that he might seem patronising. He might seem to be saying, here's Freddy back from the university to put all your little bits and pieces together. He stood there, hateful to himself, trying to find his level.

'We have to finish, you know, Freddy,' said Julia. 'It's a pity you can't sew. Everything has to be in Birmingham by tomorrow.'

'How can you get it there?' he asked. 'The last train from Blow Halt to the junction at Bishop's Leaze left at 3.47 p.m.'

'Mrs White will take it.'

'Who's Mrs White?' He felt an exile, knowing nobody.

'She comes to Evensong sometimes. She'll start for Birmingham as soon as it's night. She is driving herself in her motor.'

'Does no-one want to know – '

'It's a Panhard.'

'Does no-one want to know what I've come here for?' Fred pleaded, against the clatter of the machine. 'I believe that women ought to have the vote. I'm at a disadvantage because if I talk about anything else you'll think I'm not taking the movement seriously. I do take it seriously. But there is a decision I've come to. I want to talk to all of you about it, and Father in particular. I want to tell you about this decision I've come to.'

'You're repeating yourself,' said Hester.

'Yes, but we know he can't help it,' said Julia, strongly snipping and pinning. Fred had never seen the four women in such harmony. Perhaps their love for him, in which he had felt secure, had after all been only a by-product of their irritation with each other. Particularly that might have been true of Mrs Burden, the trusted grumbler and confidante, the secret giver of jam tarts made for him alone out of left-over scraps of pastry.

'Is Father in his study?' he asked.

'Of course,' said Julia. 'He wouldn't come in here. He knows what we're all doing, but he's frightened.'

Fred went to his father's study. Without sitting down, or introducing any kind of corrected argument, he began to explain himself in broken phrases. His father held out his hand, and he took it, feeling it chilly in the summer heat and insubstantial against his own. His father said : 'When you told me that you wanted to study Natural Sciences at university, which led, fortunately I suppose, to your present appointment, I took it for granted that you would sooner or later come to the conclusion that you had no further use for the soul. All I ask is that you shouldn't talk to me about it. The women of the house, as perhaps you have seen, for all practical purposes have deserted us.'

'I don't think they really have, Father. They're interested in what they're doing, but that's not the same thing.'

'Freddy, I'm told that there are left-overs in the larder. Have you any idea what to do with left-overs?'

'You don't have to do anything with them. They're left over from whatever was done to them before.'

His father smiled and sighed.

Chapter Six

THE DISOBLIGERS' SOCIETY

It was because he had no further use for the soul, of course, that Skippey had fastened on him and was making him go out tonight and speak under these absurd conditions. He looked, as he had been doing for some time, at the sheet of paper, on which the motto *Estoy in mis trece* was stamped in pale red. Underneath that, Dear Miss Saunders. It was now too late to write what he had intended to say, and he turned out the lamp, put on his Burberry and went down and out again to liberate his bicycle from the terribly cramped conditions of the shed.

The university societies held their meetings in various colleges, but never in St Angelicus. The Disobligers met in the Hon Secretary's Rooms, wherever they happened to be, and Skippey's rooms were in Jesus, where he tutored in experimental physics. Skippey was loved for his anxiety. His concern for details – not only physical ones, but for the least shade of feeling or lack of feeling – made others, by comparison, feel calm. And there were moments during these evenings when Skippey was an exceptionally happy man, because, for a short time at least, nothing could be seen to be going wrong, and no-one, to all appearances, was dissatisfied. But the moments of equilibrium were few, because Skippey was one of those people who by nature are incapable of running anything. Still he was hospitable. Bottles and glasses shone gently in the gas-light, with plates of Health Biscuits. Fred was late, and reproved himself. He had spent perhaps half an hour over not writing his letter, and quite ten minutes in not being able to think what to say at the meeting. And Charles Reding, who was proposing the motion, had finished speaking already. It seemed that, cruelly embarrassed at the prospect of treating immortality as a joke, he had spoken in a voice so low that it could scarcely be heard, and then sat down without explanation. He was being offered, when Fred came in, a cup of cocoa, which he accepted, only he would like a little water with it.

'Warm water, if you have it,' said poor Reding.

'He shouldn't have been asked to do this,' Skippey said quietly to Fred. 'His speech didn't go well. He didn't throw himself into it. I'm glad you've come. I shall introduce you next, and you must throw yourself into it.'

There was a slight disturbance as the door opened, knocking over the only empty chair. George Holcombe came in, a bearded figure in a red tie, for he thought of himself as a democrat. He breathed cold and wet, a discordant newcomer, struggling with the fallen chair as if it had been put there to trip him up.

'My name is Holcombe. I'm looking for Fred Fairly.'

'Are you a member of the society?'

'I paid a term's subscription to it once, several years ago. Before your day I think. I've never been to a meeting. I shall make up now for all the evenings when I forgot to come.'

'Well, Fairly's here, but he's just about to speak. Not, I'm afraid, the ideal moment – '

But Holcombe had seen Fred and shouldered his way across until he stood close to him, almost rasping him with his beard. He said hoarsely, 'To continue with what I was saying – '

'I don't want to see you, Holcombe. How did you know I was here?'

'I went to your room and read your letters. It didn't take long, as you don't seem to receive many.'

Fred remembered now that he hadn't, this second time, signed himself out.

'My own note broke off, you remember, at "there seems no point in your getting to know any young women at all". Well, I should have added "young women of the marriage-able class".'

'Sit down, Mr Holcombe,' said Skippey, with quite unexpected sharpness.

The other treasurer pointed out that it was a rule of the Disobligers that anyone could interrupt and contradict anyone else at any time.

'Not on a term's subscription made several years ago,' said Skippey. 'It can't have been more than one and six-pence at that time.'

'I shall take this up with Fairly later,' said Holcombe. 'As long as he bears in mind, *of the marriageable class*.' He took out and lit a briar pipe whose smoke joined other smoke clouds in the room where the air was foundering with burned tobacco.

'Fellow Disobligers,' Skippey persevered, 'the next speaker, Fred Fairly, opposes the motion. He was once a Christian, he tells me, but is one no longer. He might say, with Sir Leslie Stephen, that "I now believe in nothing, but I do not the less believe in morality etcetera, etcetera, and I mean to live and die a gentleman if possible."'

'Chairman, I disoblige,' said Fred. 'I don't want to be associated with Leslie Stephen, I don't know what he meant by etcetera, etcetera, and I don't wish either to live or to die like a gentleman.'

'Who was Leslie Stephen?' asked Holcombe, raising the stem of his pipe.

Skippey, ignoring both interruptions, went on. 'Fred Fairly holds, as I do, that we have no supernatural protectors or supernatural enemies. All that we can do has to be done by ourselves, and for ourselves, on this earth where we find ourselves placed. Afterwards, I mean after our present bodily life is over, there is nothing, or rather we have no reason and no right to expect anything.'

'Could you repeat the actual words of the motion?' asked a mild-sounding voice from the very back of the room. Why the distinguished Provost of St James's should be attending this meeting, Skippey couldn't imagine, although Dr Matthews, tireless and benevolent, made a point of subscribing to all the University's societies and showing an interest, from time to time, in them all. Among the attentive pipe-smokers he was the only one in full evening dress. The Disobligers were Bohemians and dressed informally, while Holcombe was wearing, under his college gown, an old green frock-coat and checked trousers.

Holding up the order paper to give himself confidence, Skippey read out: 'That the soul does not exist, has never existed, and that it is not desirable that it should exist.'

'The human soul,' said Dr Matthews.

'Yes, Provost.'

'Thank you. Unfortunately, although of course I listened to the proposer, I wasn't very well able to follow him.'

Dr Matthews was known as a man of unclouded faith.

'I didn't bargain for this,' Fred told Skippey quietly.

'I didn't bargain for Holcombe.'

'Fellow members,' Fred began. 'I'm here, as our Chairman has repeatedly pointed out, to defend the soul. To do this, I have in the first place to show that everything in life can't be referred back to physical causes. Lord Nelson, like a number of people who have undergone the amputation of a limb, continued to feel pain in his lost arm. There was no arm there, but there was a pain in the arm. This he took to be a clear indication that there are things which are beyond the explanation of the physical, or, as he called it, the corporeal.'

He paused, seeing that Skippey, who had stationed himself by now at the other end of the room, was silently raising the stem of his pipe, indicating that the intellectual tone ought to be raised. Fred, though easy-going, felt annoyed.

'The Chairman seems to be indicating that you don't want to hear anything more about Nelson's missing arm. I accept the wishes of the meeting. Let me pass to another point. There may be some here, in fact quite a number, who will tell me that every hope, every feeling, even what we think of as imagination – all of these are conditioned by organic processes. When your memory begins to slip, the cells of the cortical layers will be visibly atrophied. If you go mad, the cortical layer under the frontal bones will be darkened. Depressed, and there will be pathological changes in the upper and hind lobes. Thought is blood, you'll say to me. You are what your body is. It's inconceivable to think that the mind can survive without it. Still, which of you here hasn't been through some confrontation, some danger, or if not danger some intense and extreme personal and emotional crisis, a letter, perhaps, which you have to write, when you have been driven to argue with yourself, to say "go on, there's nothing for a rational human being to fear"? And your body will reply "Yes, there is." – "Well, even if there is, it's your duty, it's necessary for your self-respect, to go on." – "No, it isn't." – The voice, fellow members, of your adrenal gland. The body, then, has a mind of its own. It must follow, then, that the Mind has a body of its own, even if it's like nothing that we can see around us, or have ever seen.'

Fred caught a flash of light from Dr Matthews' black-rimmed spectacles behind which, as he turned his head, his eyes for a moment looked quite blank. He nodded slightly. The effect, meanwhile, of putting forward opinions which he regarded as absolute nonsense was having a curious effect on Fred. It was like hanging upside down or breathing the wrong element, water instead of air and pipe-smoke. There was a gasping, a craving for his own habitat.

'And if we agree, as we must do, that the mind has time and again shown its independence of the body and all that the body can do to it, isn't it reasonable to believe that it may do so once again, by surviving death under its own steam?' He corrected this. 'I mean, through its inability to die? But I said "isn't it reasonable?" I used the word "reasonable" – I appealed, as a scientist, and a scientist in the University of

Cambridge, to your reason. This evening, however, that is the very last thing I want to do. "We should have spoken earlier, prayed for another world absolutely, before this world was born." But we didn't do so, and now here we are, straining ourselves to make sense of the world we've got through the operations of reason. Fellow-members and Disobligers, I reject reason. I stand here this evening as a believer. I believe in gravitation without weight, life without organic matter, thought without nervous tissue, voices and apparitions without known cause, water turned into wine, stones rolled back without motive power, and souls without bodies. More than that, I believe that the grass is green because green is restful to the human eye, that the sky is blue to give us an idea of the infinite, and that blood is red so that murder will be more easily detected and criminals will be brought to justice. Yes, and I believe that I shall live forever, but I shall live without reason.'

Skippey's pipe was now moving neither up nor down, but in wide arcs from side to side. But at the same time Holcombe, who appeared to have been listening intently, stretched up both arm and pipe to register a strong disobligation.

'I'm sure that the speaker doesn't intend to confuse us or to confuse himself. But I must ask him – does he consider the soul and the mind as identical, or as different and distinct?'

It was perhaps the clearest remark that Holcombe had ever managed to make. But Skippey advanced from the back of the room, and for some reason putting his arm round Fred, said: 'As Chairman and Hon. Secretary, I claim the right to answer the question. To imagine anything means to make a new junction between two currents of activity going along two or more nerve-tracks. Electric impulses would, perhaps, be a more exact analogy than railway tracks. The origin of these currents must always be one of the sensory nerves – let us say the eye. Fairly, perhaps, sees a bird flying over the fens, and he looks attentively at a young woman, and he combines the two of them and imagines an angel. That is how the imagination works. However, no two people see the external world in exactly the same way. To every separate person a thing is what he thinks it is – in other words, not a thing, but a think.'

'That doesn't answer my question or any other question,' Holcombe cried. But the Provost of James's rose to his feet, silently communicating silence.

'Gentlemen, I'm well aware of the freedom of discussion which is allowed, by right, to the private debating societies of this University. But I little thought that I should sit here this evening, or indeed on any evening, and hear the human soul described as a think.'

He looked deliberately round from face to face.

'Although I may be out of order in speaking from the audience, I should like to put one more question to your chairman. It is this. Would you consider what I call the "inner eye" which opens for some of us, though not always when we want it or expect it – would you consider the inner eye as one of the sensory nerves?'

'Not for the purposes of dissection,' said Skippey miserably.

It was the custom after the debate, which seemed to have been pretty well knocked on the head, to offer everybody the refreshments they particularly didn't want. This was agreed to be good for the mind which, whether or not it is dependent on the body, requires constant sharpening in the form of opposition, contradiction and surprise. Skippey was in despair. What could be good for Dr Matthews' mind? For the first time it struck him that there might conceivably be something childish about the proceedings of the society. The treasurer was pressing Health Biscuits on everybody. They clattered as they struck the plates.

'I'm going back now, to smoke one more pipe, or perhaps half a pipe,' Dr Matthews said. 'Is anyone walking my way?'

He looked directly at Fred, who was not sorry to go. Certainly, not quite my way, but glad of the excuse for a walk. He helped the Provost on with his overcoat and gown. It would have been easier (as always) for him to put them on himself. 'Helping' would only be an improvement if human arms, like the arms of coats, folded backwards.

'Good-night, Mr Skippey. You must excuse me. I make it a rule to go to bed before midnight.'

The rain and the wind had both died down, leaving a ragged sky. As they started off at a sober pace towards King's Parade, the Provost remarked: 'Your name is Fairly, isn't it? I think you were in Hall at St Angelicus, when we were discussing the mystery of your south-west door. I liked what you said about the mind being entitled, as it surely is, to a body of its own, a good deal more satisfactory than the present one.'

'I wonder, Provost,' said Fred, 'if anyone's quite explained to you the objects of our Society. I mean, whoever gets up to propose the motion, and of course whoever opposes it – '

'People will go to such curious lengths,' the Provost went on, gently beating time with one hand, as though to music. 'My sister writes that she has left instructions in her will that her little finger is to be severed before her funeral so that there will be no possibility, or let us call it likelihood, of her being buried alive.' Fred was not quite sure of the right answer. – 'That should do the trick,' he said. – 'Yes, and of course she must please herself with these matters, but it's the particularity of it, Fairly – I am right about your name, I think? – I mean, one might, I think, lose one's little finger at any time. So many things are mechanised now which weren't so formerly. They provide unexpected dangers.' He added, 'As to being buried alive, so many things walk, you know, when they seem to be buried safely enough.'

What a strange face was his, protective and fatherly in the light, then again, as his head turned and his black-rimmed spectacles glittered, a blank. 'By the way, who was that man, your friend, or enemy, with a beard?'

'He's called George Holcombe.'

'I'm afraid I can't identify him. He is a Fellow of . . . ?'

'He isn't a Fellow anywhere,' said Fred. 'He's a demonstrator at the new chemistry labs.'

'He looked disturbed, I thought.'

'Perhaps he is disturbed.'

'Why so?'

Fred did not like to explain, and the Provost said reflectively, 'I always consider that the new laboratories were a mistake, but it never occurred to me that the staff were not sane.'

He fell silent and Fred began again. 'I was just going to explain to you about the way things work at the Disobligers' – but they had arrived at the Lodge, and a butler opened the door, followed by a large tabby cat which sprang up on the Provost's shoulder, digging its claws into his gown and defending its place against all comers.

'You're coming in, I hope, for that pipe?'

Fred said he was afraid he didn't smoke.

'You mean, of course, that you do,' said the Provost, stroking his cat triumphantly.

When he was back in his room Fred found that the fire was still burning pretty well. He lit the Aladdin, and tore up the letter which he had started before the meeting. On a new sheet of paper he started again: 'Dear Daisy'.

Chapter Seven

WHO IS DAISY?

If Holcombe had walked in at that moment, and asked 'Who is this Daisy, does she belong to the marriageable classes?', Fred couldn't have answered him. He knew her name and how he had come to meet her. He didn't know either who she was, or her address, and therefore he had no immediate way of sending her this letter or any other. He must, presumably, have written it for the pleasure of seeing her name on the paper.

Three weeks ago, three weeks before the Disobligers' meeting, he had been bicycling along the Guestingley Road, this time in twilight just turning into darkness.

Towards the outskirts Cambridge ceased to hold its own as a market town. Patches of field and common appeared, and, along the road, largish houses. It was getting on for dinner time. Lights appeared on the ground floors and at the same time at the top of the house, where the beds were being turned down, and the children put to bed. He saw one or two of them looking out of the windows from behind their safety bars, then the curtains were drawn, cheaper ones in the nurseries, so that the nightlight shone through, showing their colours, blue, green, brown, red. There was a good deal of traffic on the road, a number of motor cars, some farm carts. After the crossing it thinned out. Fred was able to go ahead fast. There were only two cyclists in front of him, two red tail-lamps, not together. One of them a woman, a young woman probably, the shape of one anyway, in a raincoat probably made of American cloth, which glistened in what light there was. Fred, of course, knew the road, but he was paying attention. The brick wall to the left disappeared and became a large dark gap. The gap, Fred remembered, was a farmyard gate and the farm was one of several that obstinately remained, confounding with its clatter and its fierce thin stench the respectable houses on either side of it. Fred was just on the tail of the two bikes ahead of him, possibly rather closer than he should have been, when without warning a horse and cart came lumbering almost at a canter out of the opening. It had no lights and the driver was not holding the reins but either drunk, dead or asleep, lolling over the dashboard. There was a kind of shriek or scream which might have been from the horse, since even old horses make strange noises in a state of terror, then a sound like a vast heap of glass splintering as the world, for Fred jamming on the brakes, went absurdly out of the horizontal and hit him a decisive blow, as black as pitch, on the side of the head.

When Fred came to he felt terribly thirsty. Surely if it was half-time, they'd come and give him a bit of lemon. Something was buoying him up, preventing him from feeling the pain which he knew was waiting for him. He was in bed, on a yielding mattress, which showed that wherever he was it couldn't be in college. The room seemed to breathe. Something, anyway, was breathing. It was quietly lit, but enough to throw, on a wall papered with unknown flowers, the shadows of an unknown washstand with its jug and basin. Over him there was a white quilt and a white counterpane. It was very like a nursery. On top of the white counterpane six inches away from him, he could see the left hand of a young woman, large and clean with a broad gold ring on the fourth finger. He put out his hand and touched it. The gold was smooth, the skin felt rough.

Her face was turned away, but he could see a quantity of hair, a wealth of hair his mother would call it – brownish, or between red and brown, done up at the moment any old how. Her eyes were shut.

'My God, what luck,' he thought.

His mind cleared suddenly. He sat up and waited for a moment to see whether he was going to be sick, for that would not do, one couldn't make an apology, combined with an introduction, after such a beginning. Keeping as still as possible, he said : 'I owe you an explanation. My name is Frederick Fairly. I'm a lecturer in practical physics and a Junior Fellow of, of – ' He would remember the name, surely, in a moment. 'I think I have had an accident. I think you, too, have had an accident. I think you must be the young lady who was riding just in front of me.' But that was an unjustified inference. Quite possibly she lived in this house, and this was her bed.

Without moving or opening her eyes whose long light brown lashes remained closed as though it was not likely to be worth while the trouble to look at anyone, she answered: 'I'm Daisy Saunders. Where's my cycle?'

'I don't know where it is, Mrs Saunders.'

'I'm not . . .' she said. 'I don't . . . I'm not . . . it's not mine.'

'Do you want me to go and look for it?'

She whispered, 'Yes.'

'I don't know where my bike is either, or my clothes.'

His head was bandaged. What about his vest, shirt, stiff collar, socks, sock-suspenders, trousers? 'No, I'm sorry to say I seem to have nothing at all. Otherwise I could manage to get up, I think.'

'Don't worry about your clothes. I've seen hundreds like you before.'

She's drifting, he thought. She can't know what she's saying. Doing the least sensible thing, he got out of bed. Accustomed by now to the dim light, he saw that it was a nursery, or perhaps had once been one. There was a large rocking-horse by the window, with some dark heap draped over its back which might be his trousers. Round the top of the walls ran a frieze of bluebirds in flight. The night-light was burning in a kind of metal case, a bird-cage. It's like a play, he thought. Perhaps I'm reborn. But at home he never remembered sleeping in a nursery. The girls were all in there, and although he was the oldest, he'd grown up in the box-room. 'Get back into bed, and don't move again' said the young woman. 'That's orders.'

'I'm afraid you may be losing grip, Mrs Saunders.'

'I'm not Mrs Saunders.'

Fred got back into the bed. There was a faint, delicious scent of Pears soap. The pain was worst on his right side, the right of his head, and the right shoulder, not his right leg, that seemed much as usual.

'Couldn't you find your things?'

'I don't know.'

She lifted her head a little and let it fall again.

'It's just my luck to be stuck in bed with a lazy fellow.'

Fred felt deeply shocked. In all his life he had never been called lazy before.

'Where's the fellow I was riding with? What happened to him?' she asked.

'I don't know what's happened to him. I don't care what's happened to him. Why are we talking about him?'

Perhaps he raised his voice a little. The door opened, and a stronger light intruded, first in a segment, then expanding across the bluebirds and the whiteness of the walls and ceiling. A head looked halfway round the door, and Fred heard a man's clear high voice, the true voice of scholarly Cambridge.

'Venetia, there are two total strangers in the nursery. One is a man, who has lost his clothes. The other is a woman, who, I think, has also lost her clothes . . .' Then, coming a little further into the room. 'This is my house, as it happens. You mustn't think me unwelcoming. My name is Wrayburn.'

It was clear that he had never been allowed to worry. That was not his work, worrying was done for him. Behind him, in fact, and into the room, came an exuberant charitable Mrs Wrayburn, fringed and tasselled like a squaw, although in pince-nez.

'Oh, my dears. I left you to sleep in peace till the doctor came.'

'They are ill?' asked Mr Wrayburn doubtfully.

'The farmer's son brought them both in. Strong arms, you know. But of course, I didn't want you to be disturbed.'

'I *have* been disturbed,' said Mr Wrayburn. 'I heard voices upstairs. Why didn't they take them into the farm?'

'Mrs Wrayburn?' said Fred.

'Ah, he can speak!'

'He was speaking much louder just now, and tramping about,' said Mr Wrayburn.

'It's Mr Fairly, isn't it? I found a visiting card in the top pocket of your jacket. And your wife.'

'I'm not Mrs Fairly,' said Daisy.

'Well, but your wedding ring, my dear. And you were together in a heap on the road. You were brought in here together in a heap, you know.'

'I'm not his wife.'

Mr Wrayburn summoned his good manners.

'I hope you're quite comfortable, all the same,' he said.

Fred was moved to a nursing home in Bridge Street, or at least found himself there, with his own toothbrush and dressing-gown, sent for him from St Angelicus. That was after he'd become unconscious for the second time, said the untiring Mrs Wrayburn, making kindly enquiries in a velvet hat stitched with Assisi work. Unaccountably, Mr Wrayburn had come with her. Fred wanted to know where Miss Saunders was – 'You seem more certain of her name than she was herself,' said Mr Wrayburn.

'Are you criticising her?' Fred asked. He was determined to get up and leave this place, which he couldn't afford anyway.

'Criticising her? Of course he isn't!' Mrs Wrayburn cried. 'Why should a young woman, or any woman, have to account for her comings and goings? Why should she know her name if she doesn't want to? All that we have the right to ask is, do the higher elements in her nature predominate? Are her feet on the path that leads to joy? Is she in harmony with the new century?'

'I'm not quite certain, Mrs Wrayburn,' said Fred. 'What did she say herself?'

'She didn't appear to be seriously hurt. But I thought she looked very pale. At any rate, she got up and dressed and said that she would go to a doctor if necessary as soon as she got back to London. She thanked us – not that we expected thanks –'

'We did expect them,' said Mr Wrayburn. 'I never remember expecting them more.'

'I can't thank you enough myself,' said Fred. 'Did she mention what part of London she was going to?'

Mrs Wrayburn shook her head, and with a smile of real kindness put a paper bag full of grapes and a pair of silver-plated grape-scissors by the bed. 'Snip to your heart's content, Mr Fairly, and bring them back whenever it suits you. Snip! Snip!'

As they left, Mr Wrayburn lingered behind for a moment and said, 'I learn that you are a Fellow of Angelicus. If my wife had known that she would not, of course, have made the mistake of thinking you a married man.'

The Wrayburns had notified the police. But by the time a constable arrived the horse had manoeuvred the cart to the edge of the road and was cropping the grass in the darkness, while the driver, whoever he had been, had completely disappeared. The farmer described this man as a casual, who was supposed to be going to pick up a load of old wooden sleepers at the railway station. He'd called in to collect some seed potatoes to exchange for the sleepers. The farmer couldn't say exactly what he'd intended to do with the sleepers, but they were handy things to have about the place. The man was called Saul, but that could be either his Christian name, couldn't it, or his surname. Didn't know where he came from, didn't know his cart hadn't any lights. At the station, the staff knew nothing about any sale or exchange of old sleepers which were, of course, the property of the Great Eastern Railway. All this the police regarded as unsatisfactory. Fred's bicycle, and Daisy's, both damaged, were still by the side of the road. Daisy's had been hired that morning from Trimmer's shop in Silver Street, when she had given her name and left a sovereign deposit. She hadn't been back to the shop since, and though they always took addresses as a general rule, they couldn't find any trace of hers. Fred was asked whether he had noticed anyone else on the scene at the time of the accident. Yes, another man, bicycling just in front of Miss Saunders, but he couldn't describe him and had no idea where he'd got to. This, too, the police, although they spoke much more politely than to the farmer or to Trimmer, considered unsatisfactory. It was clearly going to be difficult to prepare a case to go before the magistrate's court.

'But you'll have to find Miss Saunders,' said Fred. 'Surely there can't be anything more important than that.'

The police said that they would be making every effort to trace the young woman. But this didn't satisfy Fred. He didn't want Daisy traced, he wanted her found.

Part Two

Chapter Eight

DAISY

Daisy lived in south London, where Stockwell turns into Brixton. She had always been used to there being too many people. The pavements, in fact, seemed too small to hold the houses' inhabitants, so that they spilled into the gutters and stood there offering objects for sale – matches, penny toys made of lead or tin, almanacs, patent medicines, cage-birds and so on, until darkness fell and the last prospect vanished. Then the house doors opened and somehow took them all in, along with the day's returning workers, the preachers from the gas-lit street-corners, the children, the drunks, all in and battened down at last. But south London, once you got away from the river and its warehouses, was built low, so that whenever the fog cleared, you saw an immense sky, moving at its own pace through sun and cloud, or over the net of the stars.

Daisy grew up with the smells of vinegar, gin, coal smoke, paraffin, sulphur, horse-dung from backyard stables, chloride of lime from backstreet factories, and baking bread every morning. When she was quite young they had been very poor. That was bad, but on the other hand, the great city was almost as well adapted to serve the very poor as the very rich. The stalls in the markets were strictly arranged, with all the cheapest stuff at one end. The customers accepted, without pretensions, which end they belonged to. At the cheap end you could get cow-heel, which didn't turn as quickly as most kinds of meat. The cow-heel simmered murkily at the back of the range for most of the day, until the broth, according to Mrs

Saunders, thickened of its own accord. After the long boil you took the bones out and pressed the glutinous grey mass under a plate weighed down by a flat iron on top of it. One of the glue factories down by the river came round collecting the bones, although they paid very little for used cow-heels.

On quarter-days a hand-bill came through every letter-box: *Keep ahead of your landlord. Late night work not objected to.* These men would move your stuff in a barrow, which made less noise than a pony-cart. The Saunderses, mother and daughter, always circled round their home ground, never taking rooms twice in the same street. Daisy's mother wanted to stay close to her job at the Falcon Brewery. Daisy minded babies. She had no brothers or sisters of her own, but that was an advantage, otherwise she'd have got sick and tired of babies by this time, Mrs Saunders said.

It stood to reason that Daisy had had a father, but she couldn't give a connected account of him. He was down on her birth certificate as a packer and handler. What had he ever packed or handled, where was he handling now? Neither mother nor daughter wanted to know this. Then came an unexpected, indeed inconceivable change of fortune when Mrs Saunders' sister, never before referred to, left her a house, a small terrace house in Hastings. Solicitors wrote to say that they had been "directed" to tell her this, and "desired" to give her the particulars. 'But I thought she was dead,' Mrs Saunders said, again and again.

'Well, she is now,' said Daisy, 'so you can count yourself right.'

'And if she'd been alive I always thought she'd gone to live in New South Wales.'

'Don't grieve,' said Daisy. 'You're not as sorry as all that.'

'If I'd been given time I'd have been sorry,' said Mrs Saunders.

The news was not quite as inconceivable as it had seemed. The solicitor wrote again, desiring to correct the impression (which no-one but himself had given) that the house be-

longed, or would ever belong, to Mrs Saunders. She had been
left the end of a lease, sub-let. For the next five years, only,
they would receive £5 a quarter. That will make a great
difference to your way of life, the solicitor told them.

Mrs Saunders continued bottle-capping at the Falcon,
because it entitled her to send her daughter to the Licensed
Victuallers' Free School in Latchmere Road. Daisy grew up to
be tall and slender, but solid. She had substance to her. Life
would get a lot of work out of her. Until it turned grey her hair,
recklessly curling, would always attract attention, because of
the difficulty of deciding whether it was more brown than red.
It was all according to the light.

At fifteen she put her hair up, securing it with strong steel
pins, and started as a clerical. That meant crossing the river,
along with a hundred and fifty thousand other south
Londoners, twice a day. The journey was compared at that
time by sociological observers to a great war or catastrophe in
a neighbouring land from which the fugitives, forbidden to
look back, scurried over the river bridges by any means
available to them, only checked by the fear of falling
underfoot. At the tram stop there were no queues – queues
were for free medical dispensaries only – and when the tram
lurched round the corner, drawing up sharply, the crowd
rolled onto it and with it like a dark swarm of bees. You had to
attack and be among the first. But defence, too, had to be
studied. Daisy went out to work like her friends, closely
buttoned, hat-pinned, and corseted against unwanted ap-
proaches. She also wore on her wedding finger a broad gold
ring, which had come to her from the long unsuspected aunt in
Hastings. Had Aunt Ellie ever married? Inside it was an
inscription – *Whatever there is to know, That we shall know one
day*.

Those who did the approaching, in the stifling proximity of
the tram, were inclined not to believe in the wedding-ring, and
knew what else Daisy was wearing as well as she did. It was a
battle with no accepted rules and when the tram began to roll

with its plunging, strong-smelling human freight, men put
their hands over their ticket and money pockets while
schoolboys protected their genitals and women every point of
contact, fore and aft.

Daisy had been taken on at Lambert's Glazing Supplies, in
Fulham. Dark and unpromising-looking as the warehouse
was, it had over its entrance a large stained glass pane
representing the Finding of the Lost Sheep. The sky had been
cut out of a single piece of opalescent glass in which white and
blue had been fused together at random, giving the effect of
high summer clouds. Probably no-one in England, in the year
1909, could have produced a panel like this one; certainly
Lambert's couldn't. Although almost every small house in
Battersea, Clapham, Streatham and Stockwell had its bit of
coloured glass over the front door, Daisy had never seen,
either before or in church, anything quite like it before.

The hours at Lambert's were from eight until eight. Young
Daisy arrived with the irrepressible readiness to please, as
though on creation's first morning, which is one of the earth's
great spectacles of wasted force. She was given a stool and a
peg in an almost lightless and airless tank behind the glass-
store. The columns of figures were a delight to her, particularly if some of them had gone astray. The sight of 8073 foot of
glazing at one shilling and sixpence a foot, with quarter-inch
lead bars, subsequently changed to five-sixteenths, and the
whole estimate to be raised by $13\frac{1}{2}$% gave her satisfaction, as
though she had faced defiance and quelled it.

She was earning twelve shillings a week. Mrs Saunders lost
her job at the brewery. There was something wrong with her,
a pain, not always in the same place. She had the time now to
think about it. They had moved into two nice airy rooms on
the top floor of a house where the handwritten cards, in every
window except theirs, offered useful services. Plain Washing
Taken In (this was on the ground floor, where the boiler was),
Music Correctly Taught, Herbal Remedies. 'You don't want
to try those,' said Daisy. But Mrs Saunders had already been

to pass the time of day with the herbalist. She was able to report that he had nothing but doses of groundsel, for bringing it on, and penny royal, in plain envelopes, for bringing it off. Nothing for a woman of her age.

After less than a year, Daisy handed in her notice at Lambert's, and started a new job, still in clerical, at Sedley's Cartons. That, too, did not last many months. Had there been anything wrong with her work? No, said Daisy, unmoved, they couldn't fault her there. Mrs Saunders sighed. 'Well, you told me Mr Lambert couldn't keep his hands to himself. Didn't he take any notice of poor Ellie's wedding-ring?' 'Lord, mother, that's only for the tram,' said Daisy. 'It's just for travelling. I take it off at work. Lambert knows I'm fifteen, and he knows I'm not married. We won't talk about Lambert any more.'

'What about Mr Sedley?'

'He's worse,' said Daisy. 'He's carny.'

'Carny' was a word which nobody in London south of the river used lightly. Nobody, either, would have thought of Daisy as difficult, or hard to suit, or even particular. She was, on the contrary, generous, and described as the kind of girl who'd give you the teeth out of her head, if she could get them loose. It was only that she didn't want decisions made for her by old Mr Lambert, still less by young Sedley.

There were a lot of people out of work now, more than she ever remembered. She made out she was a school-leaver, and got a recommendation from Father Haggett at the Anglo-Catholic Mission church of St James the Less. He felt for his parishioners, and was ready to sign anything, within reason, to help them to earn. With this she got a washing-up job, but at seven shillings a week only, with threepence held back in case of breakages.

Daisy loved her mother, who was the only relative she had, but she supposed it might be said that she killed her. In the spring of 1909 the Selfridge Department Store opened in Oxford Street. A circular was printed – everyone saw it, because it was posted up in every window. Daisy read it in the Women's Penny Reading Room at the back of the church hall. 'We wish it to be clearly understood that our invitation to the opening of Selfridge's, is to the whole British public and to visitors from overseas – that no cards of admission are required – that all are welcome – and that the pleasures of shopping as well as those of sight-seeing begin from the Opening Hour. Everything is NEW except the splendid old time-tried principles that must govern it – integrity, sincerity, liberality in dealing and courteous service.'

The magnificent building, with its columned frontage and pillared vistas, had gone up, said the circular, within a year, employing fifteen hundred men during this sad time of depression. There were lifts, worked by electricity. 'I'll take you to have a look at it if you like,' Daisy told her mother. 'It'll be my half-day.' Mrs Saunders had been up to the West End often enough, but never into a large store. The notion of going there under the wing of her tall, good-looking daughter drove her nearly crazy with joy, but she did not drop her defences.

'I don't mind, if you happen to be going that way,' she said.

They took a tram to Victoria, and then the open-top motor-bus, nipping up the stairs like larks ascendant to get the two front seats on the left-hand side where they would see most, defying the dark greyish clouds to break. Oxford Street was almost at a standstill, blocked with horses and motors. They got out at Ruscoe's, the humble draper's next to the new great store, at No. 424. A red carpet covered the pavement, in homage to Selfridge's customers. Even the humble ones who wanted to go into Ruscoe's trod at least on the edge of this carpet. Inside the main door, blazing with light, Gordon Selfridge himself patrolled in a frock coat, exchanged, when darkness fell, for full evening dress. Mrs Saunders regally nodded to him. With Daisy to take her arm, she felt subservient to none. In fact, what was joyous to her was not the thought of the hundred departments, freely compared in the store's advertisements to the bazaars of the farthest orient, or the twelve hundred assistants, but the chance of showing them that, to a woman like herself, they were not so much.

After they had seen perhaps twenty of the hundred departments, Daisy suggested taking the lift up to the Tea Gardens. The Gardens were on the roof of the building. They could do with some fresh air. Daisy said this as though both of them had just come up from the depth of the country, from green woods or potato fields.

'Air!' said Mrs Saunders. 'They can't make us pay for that.'

'We haven't paid for anything yet,' said Daisy.

In these early days a bugle was to be blown every morning when Selfridge's opened, and again when it shut, as though every day spent in shopping was an epoch of history. Mrs Saunders, however, although she had talked a good deal about the promised bugle, seemed, now that she had the chance, not to care whether she heard it or not.

'I think I'll go home now,' she said. 'You can only see so much.'

'You're getting tired, mother.'

'No I'm not,' said Mrs Saunders. 'Do I ever?'

'It's not such a sin to be tired.'

'It's a great mistake to admit it, though.'

After that she said very little until they had transferred once again to the tram and crossed the river back to their own country. The market streets were dark, the stalls wheeled into the side alleys and shrouded closely in oilcloth. You could smell the cramped stables, and hear now and then a horse shut up for the night, shifting from foot to foot. Under the gaslights at the street junctions the preachers, the political speakers, the Marxists, the suffragists, had given up all hope of audiences, and gone back to whatever homes they had.

'What did you think of it, though, Daisy?' Mrs Saunders asked. 'How long do you think it'll last? Floor after floor of stuff, I didn't hardly look at how much they were asking for it. And all laid out for everyone to stare at, it didn't seem quite decent.'

'I know,' Daisy said. 'They're almost asking for people to come in and help themselves to the things.'

She took the front door key out of the pocket of her skirt.

'Well, I did take just one thing,' said Mrs Saunders.

My God, she never, Daisy thought. Still, it can't have been anything very big. She asked, 'How did you get it back here?'

'Just in the old way.' In her umbrella, then. She put her arm round her bony little mother.

'I took it for you, Daisy, as a present for you.'

'No, you didn't,' said Daisy.

'Well, perhaps not.'

It turned out, when they got upstairs, to be a 'rat', a roll of artificial hair over which you combed your own, to make it look luxurious enough for the present style. Unfortunately, the rat usually showed through to some extent, and this one was of a golden yellow shade.

'Do you really like it?' Daisy asked doubtfully.

'No, not really. I'm not so keen on it now I look at it again. It don't match my hair and it don't match yours. It reminded me of the colour I had when I was your age. We might take it back if we go that way again.'

'I shouldn't worry, with twelve hundred assistants on top of the customers, I expect they'll find a good bit missing at the end of every day. You ought to have taken something you really wanted.'

Three days later Mrs Saunders died, while Daisy was out at work. She felt the loss through and through, and, even more keenly, the thought that she hadn't been there to take charge. She did not ask the doctor whether the outing to the West End could have brought on the heart attack because she knew he wouldn't be able to give a definite answer either way. Therefore she said nothing about it.

The herbalist, the teacher of correct music, and the taker-in of plain washing all found their way to Daisy's room, where the washstand was, and the oil stove, both curtained off. They had come, as she very well knew, to see if there was going to be anything to spare from her mother's things. She told them that after she'd seen to the arrangements, they could come and see what there was. She wasn't going to keep anything except one photograph of her mother as a young woman. It didn't suggest that Mrs Saunders had ever had golden hair, but then the photographer, when he did the tinting, might have got that wrong.

'Not keeping the furniture, Miss Saunders?' the herbalist asked.

'I'm not staying here,' said Daisy.

'But the washstand?'

'I shan't take it with me.' He must have worked out it was behind the curtain, or else he'd been poking round and knew it had a marble top.

She notified the solicitor, who desired to express his regret. When she called round to ask him about her Aunt Ellie's house, he pointed out that on Mrs Saunders' death, the payment of £5 quarterly automatically lapsed.

'Who gets it, then?' Daisy asked. The solicitor said that she would do well to consider her future carefully. Daisy told him that she had always wanted and still wanted, now that she didn't have her mother to consider, to be a hospital nurse.

'There are two ways of entering nursing,' he said, 'either you go in as an ordinary probationer – most probationers, I believe are from the domestic service class – or you go in to train as a lady nurse, paying a premium, and of course wearing quite a different uniform, and not being required to undertake any distasteful work. You would, I imagine, have very little contact with the lady nurses.'

He charged nothing for this advice, perhaps as a compensation for the loss of the rent from the Hastings house.

Chapter Nine

THE BLACKFRIARS HOSPITAL

The matron at Blackfriars interviewed applicants only between two and four o'clock on Fridays. When Daisy had rung the bell and been admitted through the outer and inner doors, she braced herself to measure up to the other applicants. She was wearing a navy-blue coat and skirt and a navy-blue straw hat painted over with a patent lacquer so that it would keep its shape even in quite heavy rain. Two pins with plain glass heads secured it. The sleeves of her costume were rather short. She had had to turn them up a bit to hide the wear on the cuffs. Some inked them in, but Daisy never. On the inner door there was a painted notice which read 'This hospital turns away more than a thousand applications a year from persons desiring to train as nurses. Every year perhaps 4 or 5 are accepted.' – Words of challenge, welcome to the free spirit. Because or in spite of them, every chair in the waiting-room was occupied. Daisy stood with her back to the wall, looking at the stiffly sitting girls. All wore navy-blue costumes, all the sleeves were unnaturally short, all wore straw hats with the exception of one dark, foreign-looking woman, perhaps Spanish, perhaps from Gibraltar, older than the others. You couldn't apply over the age of thirty-eight; perhaps she was thirty-seven. She asked Daisy if she had come far. Daisy said she was used to walking. The others looked away, as though, if they listened, conscience might drive them to offer her a seat.

'The next one will soon be out,' said the dark woman. 'She is not taking long today.'

'Have you been here before, then?' Daisy asked, but that

was not an acceptable question, and there was no answer. The white-painted brass-locked door of the matron's office opened and a girl came out, crossed the room with head bowed, and said something (but nothing that anyone could hear) to the receptionist. All the applicants stirred a little. Either she had had a cold, or she was in tears. The porter was called; the receptionist told him to get a cab. A lady applicant, perhaps.

Daisy was the last to be called. She looked with respect at the woman sitting on the other side of the desk. You had to struggle, perhaps fight and bleed, to get to a position like that. Matron was short, pale and pale-haired, as straight as though suspended from a hook.

'You may sit down.'

She repeated from the application paper in front of her Daisy's name and address.

'You are nearly eighteen. Are you a single woman or a widow? If you are a widow, have you children? If children, how are they provided for?'

'I'm single.'

'And have you anyone dependent on you for support?'

'Not now.'

'You may call me Matron.'

'Not now, Matron.'

'But recently?'

'There was my mother. She died in March.'

'And that left you free to apply to enter the nursing profession, which of course would entail your living away from home.'

'I suppose it did.'

'So that her death has been release for you.'

'No, I won't say that, and I don't say that. It wasn't a release for her either.'

The matron appeared not to listen to this, but fixed her attention on the papers on her desk. 'Your birth certificate. You're too young, but the Governors have changed their policy about that to some extent. Vaccination certificate.

Height?' Daisy said she thought five foot six, without heels. 'It's not a matter of thinking,' the matron said. 'Educated at the Victuallers' School, certificate of good conduct and application. Did you study Latin? Do you understand what I mean by enemata?'

Daisy did not, but said she was prepared to learn.

'I don't expect the girls who come to us to know anything. Now, are you strong and healthy, and have you always been so? Let me explain, in order to save time, that several of the applications today mentioned, apparently only as an afterthought, that they had rheumatic fever as children, which meant that if they were accepted here they might collapse and become a nuisance and an expense at any given moment.'

'I've always been strong and healthy,' said Daisy and beneath her put-on clothes she felt her physical self-respect extend and stretch itself, like a cat in the sun.

'And your sight and hearing are perfect?'

'Yes, I think so. I've never thought about them.'

'You notice that I wear reading-glasses myself. I need them now, but as a probationer I did not need them. Have you any physical defects?'

'What kind of defects?' Daisy asked, a little troubled.

'Any that I can't see at a cursory glance. You may be subject to very heavy periods. You may be marked and scarred. Your spine may be crooked. . . . Have you any tendency to pulmonary complaints?' She looked up sharply. 'Do you understand what I mean by "pulmonary"?'

'Yes, it means to do with the lungs.'

'Pertaining to the lungs. A sickly nurse is of no use to the profession. One might call her an enemy of the profession. Above all, though, we don't want a weakly habit of constant complaint. As a rough guide, remember that while the average man is ill for four days a year, a grown woman must expect to spend one fourth of her life in actual pain.'

Daisy felt a rush of admiration. So far she herself had done nothing like her fair share.

'The next thing I am going to ask you is: have you read, and do you clearly understand, the Regulations of this hospital? I find that reading and understanding are not the same thing. Copies are handed out in the waiting-room, but although the applicants have plenty of time before their interview to go through them, they often turn out, in fact, not to have grasped them at all.'

Nobody had given Daisy a copy of the Regulations, perhaps they had run out, but to say this would get the receptionist into trouble. She made a guess.

'I'm not afraid of getting up early.'

'Or of doing the rough work in the wards? Or of taking only one week's holiday during your first year's probation?'

'No, I ain't.'

'What did you say?'

'No, I'm not, Matron.'

'You can obtain another copy of the Regulations on your way out. Meanwhile, I shall require copies of your references and in particular one from your last employer.' Daisy hesitated. 'If you haven't brought them with you in writing, you may re-present yourself with them next Friday.'

And the tiny matron nodded dismissal to the tall, strong, juicy, courageous, not quite confident young woman, who clearly had something wrong with her references. Daisy stopped in the hospital's wide porch and changed her good boots for her old ones, then began to walk, keeping her hopes low, through the bright cold afternoon streets. Presently the dark-skinned woman who had been in the waiting-room caught up with her. She must have been hanging about, waiting to say, as she now did, 'Miss, you remember me. I didn't answer your question, but I will answer it now. You asked me if I had applied at the hospital before. I have applied, but each time they would not accept me. I can't fill in the form where it says "single or widow". What can I write? You see, I am single, but I have a child.'

'Let down, were you?' asked Daisy. 'I should fill that in, if I were you.'

The woman looked at her mournfully, and said that to be young was to be without care. 'I live just near here. Perhaps you would like to step in and take a cup of tea.'

'No thank you, I better hadn't.'

'Why not, it won't take a moment.'

'No, I'd better be on my way.'

'You would come in if I was married.'

'You shouldn't have told me about it if you thought I'd object,' said Daisy, smiling. 'There was no call.'

They stopped in front of a small finishing laundry, where the shirts were brought in rough-ironed from a bigger place, to have the collars done. 'I am known here as Mrs Martinez.'

'Why not?' said Daisy.

Mrs Martinez walked across the laundry with only a nod to the woman in charge. Out of a wicker washing-basket on the counter she lifted a child of about two years old who had been sitting in it playing with a handful of dolly-pegs. You'd never get an English child to sit quiet like that.

'My word, is that yours?' said Daisy. 'What a love. I'd have thought it would have been a bit older.'

'I am more than thirty-five years of age,' said Mrs Martinez, 'but unfortunately it seems that I am still fertile.'

'So I see,' said Daisy. 'You ought to know better by this time.' She held out her arms and took the baby, preventing it with a gentle movement from pulling out her hatpins. 'You don't want to let things upset you.'

'We fertiles are the unlucky ones,' said Mrs Martinez. 'However, there will be a time when thirty-five won't seem old to you.'

'I shan't let that upset me either. I shan't be upset, let's say, in 1939.' They both laughed, the date sounded absurd. They were on the way upstairs, stopping on the half-landing, where there was a fish-tail gas jet and a sink.

74

Through the back window Daisy could see a very small yard, with a tap, and a pump for when the tap failed.

Above the yard walls there was a segment of dazzling sky, drifting down with bright silvery clouds. 'I should think you'd like looking out at this,' she said, 'when there's no fog.' But it seemed that Mrs Martinez came from a part of Spain where coal was mined, and the sky was hazy all the year round. Only the fogs made her feel at home in London. Daisy handed back the little boy, bundled up in his petticoats. 'I won't stay any longer, Mrs Martinez.' She could see that every drop of water would have to be fetched up by some means or other, from the yard. Every cup of tea would be a burden.

'I'm sorry you have to go. I should like to talk more. We might have talked about the sorrows of women.'

Daisy paused, two steps down.

'But if you're going,' said Mrs Martinez, 'I wonder if you could oblige me.'

'Did you mean – '

'Tide me over a little, that is.'

'How much are you short, Mrs Martinez?'

'Oh, one shilling and sixpence, two shillings and sixpence.'

'Don't you know which?' asked Daisy.

'No, I don't know which,' said Mrs Martinez, who appeared to be laughing.

'Is there anyone pressing you for payment, anything like that?'

Daisy usually kept her purse in her inner breast pocket, but not today, when she was wearing her good costume and had to think of the line. It was in the skirt pocket, with her key. She dragged it out and extracted two shilling pieces. Mrs Martinez took them with indifference, and gave one of them to the baby to hold.

The hospital regulations, when Daisy read them at last, suggested that one of the references should be from the applicant's place of worship. 'Another recommendation, how old are you now?' asked Father Haggett. They were in the study of the cheerless clergy house. 'Seventeen, well, I'm going to write you down as bright, hard-working, honest and charitable. Shake your head if you don't like what I'm putting.' – 'I don't know about "honest",' said Daisy. 'Right and wrong are all depending, I think, so is honest.' – 'You make up your own rules about that, then,' said Father Haggett. – 'No, they're depending,' said Daisy. 'They don't change, it's what they refer to that changes.' – 'You think I'm going to argue with you, but I'm not,' said Father Haggett. 'To oblige you, I won't say you're honest. Completely dependable.' The door was thrown open and the housekeeper, standing on the threshold, said that the oxtail was ready. 'You can have it hot now or cold later. Father Smith obliged by having his earlier.'

'I am summoned,' said Father Haggett, writing a few more lines. – 'You didn't ought to be put upon like that by your housekeeper,' said Daisy. – 'You should get rid of this idea of life as a battlefield,' said Father Haggett. 'In a battle you can only succeed through fraud and violence. I shall pray for you in your new profession. Pray for me, Daisy Saunders.' Daisy thanked him while he looked through his desk drawers for an envelope.

The other necessary reference was, as she had feared, her most recent employer. She sent young Mr Sedley a letter. He did not answer, so she went to the box-factory in person, knowing that he left about half-past six, when his regular hired motor-car called for him. Sedley recognised her and asked her if she'd changed her mind. She said she hadn't, but wanted a reference. Sedley told her he didn't feel like giving her one, and she could stick that up her Khyber. He jumped into the motor, slammed the door shut, and she watched the springs bounce and shiver as he threw himself heavily into his seat. Not having wasted much time at Sedley's, she went on to Lambert's Glazing. The reception clerk at the door was a friend of hers. She was allowed straight up. With wheedling, stocking-top-fancying old Mr Lambert things went more easily. He was afraid that she had come to complain. 'Let me see, Miss Sanderson, when did you leave us exactly?' – 'I want you to make it quite clear that Miss Daisy Saunders worked satisfactorily, and that she left your employ a fortnight ago.' She felt her resolution was beginning to dissolve in pity, but persevered. 'Just do that, Mr Lambert, and you've no more worries, you'll never set eyes on me again, I give you my solemn word.' Old Mr Lambert, groping and fumbling with the slippery shapes of his ideas, struggled to keep hold. His face hung down in folds, his eyes moistened. – 'What kind of post is it that you're looking for now?' – 'I want to be a hospital nurse.' Old Lambert seemed relieved. – 'A nurse! Ah, we'll all of us be needing one of them sooner or later. You want to care for others, that's it, isn't it?' Daisy said, 'I should like to know how the human body works, and what has to be done to it when it doesn't work.' – 'You're quite wrong there, quite wrong, that's for doctors. Nurses, surely, shouldn't know how anything works. You will want to soothe, Miss Sandison, soothe and tend, and to keep the spirits up.' – 'I do want to do that,' said Daisy. – 'The mind is as important as the body,' said old Lambert, who had, perhaps, learnt this at last.

The Blackfriars accepted the references, and Daisy became Saunders. For seven weeks, until she passed her first exam, she wouldn't even be a probationer. She was advised to get herself a second-hand Kirke's, shoes a size larger than she usually wore, a good stock of underwear, and, if she could afford any extras, some scented soap, a bottle of eau-de-cologne, and a packet of cocoa or cocoatina. Kirke's was a nursing handbook. Daisy sat down with Kirke's on her last night in the room she had shared with her mother, and looked at the specimen questions.

1. What would you do to calm a restless patient?
2. What would you do in a case of syncope?

3. Should a heart case have a bath? If not, why not, and what substitute would you give?

4. What are your duties at the physician's visit?

5. How you would apply leeches? And how would you ensure their biting at the exact spot? What is the best way of telling one end of a leech from the other, and how can you induce it to vomit when the application is over, in order that it may be used again as expeditiously as possible?

On the day of her arrival the Home Nurse, absurdly overworked, showed her into a small double cubicle. On the other bed was a pile of knitted stockings, a tin of biscuits and a tin trunk. The name on the trunk was K. Smith.

'She'll have to get rid of all this rubbish,' said the Home Nurse. 'You can make a start. Put on your dress, cap and apron. No, not like that.' Probationers were to stand when a Sister spoke to them, keep their hands out of their pockets, never lean against a wall or a table, never laugh, run or talk in the corridors, and remember to call the doctors and medical students 'sir'. Only the lady pupils might call him 'doctor'.

Even these first regulations were more than Kate Smith, who turned up at last, having been lost in the corridors, could remember. At once Daisy found in her a friend who needed protection. The very first time they worked together they had to go down one of the female wards, Daisy to the right, Kate to the left, putting the patients' hair in tight pigtails; they were being got ready for their operations. Daisy finished first and looked back.

'Lord, Kate, whatever have you done to them?'

'Put them right for me, Daisy!'

And Daisy rapidly put them right for the first of many times, not knowing how dangerous generosity is to the giver.

Chapter Ten

THE MEN'S WARD

When the whole of the men's ward had been persuaded to face the morning, the patients washed, wounds dressed, the windows facing the world open an inch and a half, those away from the wind open six inches, all of them two inches less than during the night, when the gas jets were burning, the abdominal cases on their backs, the apopleptics on their face, the fractured skulls on their sides, the broken limbs raised on blocks (or at the end of the ward, where the blocks had run out, on tin bowls), the coughs hushed, the morbid curiosity about the screen cases quelled, the steak-and-kidney pudding smuggled in by No. 23 (to keep up his strength before his operation) quietly removed, and the bed-covers all smooth, all white, all blameless, all blank, all clean, there was a moment of balance and harmony, scarcely real, when nurses and probationers knew themselves as artists. Then a dark group, a black patch, began to move up the white rows that gave the hard-won illusion of peace, and at one bed or another, indicated by Matron, the consulting surgeon, with his train of students, paused. The white bed then became a place of anxiety and pain, or the memory of pain, or the expectation of it. When surgeon, Matron and students moved on, the probationers, at a respectful distance, straightened the sheets, the pillows and the coverlet and settled the patient, who had not only been frightened but was now suffering from the loss of his only few minutes of importance in the men's ward of the Blackfriars, and, perhaps, on this earth.

Daisy reproved herself, imagining that no-one else could

feel as she did. It came out that all of them did, all the probationers, all became unreasonable at the sight of the white beds, the black procession. 'We're all going daft together,' she told Kate, who said they couldn't be as crazy as Dr Sage.

Dr Sage, the Senior Registrar, was, of course, not crazy, but he was indulged. He liked to make an effect, and the habit of allowing him to do this had grown in the protected world of the hospital. Daisy had heard his voice before she had ever seen him, at the far end of the fever ward.

'All the bloodshed, Sister, caused by the warlike ambition of Napoleon is as nothing compared with the myriads of persons who have sunk into their graves from a misplaced confidence in the food value of beef-tea. As a food, it is but as the mirage of water seen by the thirsty travellers in the desert. There is no real water. So with beef-tea; it is not a food.'

Daisy had come in with the pile of clean bandages for the patients to roll. They had nothing to read or to do, and had to be kept occupied. Dr Sage, who had been addressing the Ward Sister, turned now with his stethoscope still round his neck, his grey moustache triumphant. He pointed at Daisy; it was one of his set pieces. 'You, young woman, are a probationer in your first year?'

Daisy replied that she was.

'And your name?'

'Saunders, sir.'

'You heard what I was saying to Sister Morris?'

'Yes, sir.'

'Tell me: as a child, did you drink beef-tea?'

'We used to drink the gravy, sir, from the cow-heel.'

The whole ward was watching, as at a play. Those who could, sat upright. Dr Sage shouted furiously.

'Don't make the mistake, Saunders, of thinking you kept alive on that!'

Yes, he had put her right, and the ward was satisfied. Although they loved Daisy, in whose energetic hands they felt safe, she ought, of course, not to have spoken, at least for another year, to a doctor at all. Ward Sister was prepared to overlook it on this occasion. But Dr Sage carried away the impression – a firm impression, he had no time for any others – that this probationer had failed in the first duty, repeated at the beginning of every lecture on elementary physiology, anatomy, materia medica and hygiene – the duty of absolute obedience. Saunders had not contradicted him, but she had not given him the answer he expected. Nevertheless, he believed she would make a good nurse. The patients, meanwhile, trusted Dr Sage, not because he was trustworthy, but because he had set his face against new methods, and every one of them who was allowed to take anything at all by the mouth was prescribed generous draughts of medicine from their own bottle. Down in the dispensary, the engine room of the hospital, ranged in alphabetical order, were preparations of aceta (or vinegars), aquae (or waters), balsams, confections, conserves, decoctions, enemata, essences, glycerines, infusions, hypodermic liquors, oils, pepsins, resins, spirits, succi or juices, syrups, thyroid extracts, trochisii or lozenges, unguents, vapores, vina (or wines). In the wards the kidney sufferers, waiting to sweat into their thick flared night-shirts, were dosed with nitre, squill and broom. Fever cases had a drop of aconite in a teaspoonful of water every fifteen minutes, then antimony every quarter of an hour. Babies with enteritis had tar-water and brandy. Gallstones and strangulated hernia were treated with opium, paralysis with strychnine, tapeworm with oil or male fern. Over-prescriptions brought drama to the patients' tedious day. Too much antimony made them faint, too much quinine caused buzzing in the ears, too much salicylic acid brought on delirium, too much strychnine made them unable to swallow (and they twitched violently), too much mercury made them dribble, too much iodine made them sneeze uncontrollably, with too much antifebrin their skins turned dusky blue. When they were disinfected internally with carbolic acid their urine became olive green. No matter, all, or most of these excesses could be corrected. *Fiat Mistura!* Dr Sage's bold prescriptions, many of them with rhubarb, ginger and honey added in a wild gesture of palatability, came up from the depths, where his executives pounded and mixed in bottles green, and red, which were poured out by the nurses, always keeping the labels uppermost, as they had been trained to do, and always into clean medicine-glasses inscribed with mysterious lines and numbers. The patients swallowed gladly. Their names were on the bottles. The doctor had given them something.

Chapter Eleven

THE CASE OF JAMES ELDER

On January 16th, 1912, James Elder threw himself off the Adelphi steps into the Thames. In spite of the fog he was noticed by the skipper of a sprat-boat, who held his head above the water until a passing steamer picked him up. He was put to bed at Waterloo police station, which kept a special bunk for the purpose, and given First Aid by the Sylvester's method until he could be transferred to the infirmary. But he had begun to talk deliriously and his condition had seemed too serious for the infirmary. Accordingly, the police had sent him round to the Blackfriars, in a stretcher packed with tins of various shapes filled with hot water, one under each arm, one in the groin. After he was admitted the constable waited to collect the tins, which were the property of the river police. He would be round in the morning to take down a statement and, if appropriate, make a charge of attempted suicide.

At seven minutes past two in the morning, James Elder, who had been identified by personal letters in his pocket, woke up. Night Sister in the men's ward had two post-operatives to look to. She told Daisy to keep an eye on 23, who had been admitted just before they came in. Swallowing Thames water often meant typhoid, but they wouldn't know that for a few days. Twenty-three became half-conscious and began to mutter and call out, 'Flo.' Daisy went to him, sat down by the bed and told him that she was not Flo, she was a hospital nurse and he was quite safe in the Blackfriars. 'Take my hand, Flo,' he said. 'I'm not Flo,' she repeated. 'I'm a probationer.'

'Why did you bring me in here?'

'You're not well. You've hurt your head, and you've swallowed a lot of dirty water.'

'I had to do that. You know why, Flo. If you don't know, you can ask the solicitor.'

'You have to keep calm now,' said Daisy. 'You can talk to your family in the morning.'

'I haven't any family. I haven't any money. I don't want to call you Nurse. I want to call you Miss. I want to call you the Eternal Woman. Are you ashamed of that?'

'I'm not ashamed of anything.' To quieten him down, and convince him that he was in hospital, she took his temperature, putting the thermometer back in its glass jar of Condy's Fluid. The patient complained of thirst, and became agitated when told that he mustn't, until a doctor had seen him, have anything to drink. She rubbed ice on his forehead, and held his hand when once again he cried out, 'Flo!'

'Well, tell me, what is it?'

'There's something I want to tell you.'

'Well, I'm here,' she said.

After a year and a half she had become accustomed to the things that patients wanted to tell her, particularly on night duty. Night and darkness in the hospital were a time apart, nine and a half hours, almost, of something like freedom shared with the sleepless under the thin hissing of the lowered gas.

'Swear you're listening,' he said.

'I'm listening.'

'I'm a suicide, aren't I? That's why you brought me in here. A sad case, a sad waste of brilliant promise. Yes, I took the fatal plunge. I want you to tell me something. Very earnestly, in all sincerity, I want you to tell me this: is there anything about me in the newspapers?'

Eructations, slight vomiting of mucus mixed with water.

'I don't think they're printed yet,' said Daisy.

'What time is it?'

'Four thirty-two.'

'Just between dark and dawn.'

'Not a bit of it, it's winter. It won't be light for a long time yet.'

'When the dawn comes, will it be in the morning papers?'

'I shouldn't think so.'

'When do they print them?'

'Do you mean that's all you're thinking about?'

'Yes, all I'm thinking about.'

'Think about getting better,' said Daisy. 'If you've got no family, at least you must have friends.'

'I haven't any friends.'

'Who's Flo, then?'

'Not a friend.' Daisy by now had managed to get the draw-sheet off and he lay back with his head a little on one side as though listening, then started off again. 'She might read it in the paper. When the dawn comes up like thunder she may see a headline: WAPPING CLERK ATTEMPTS FELO DE SE.'

'There's plenty of clerks in Wapping,' said Daisy. 'Wapping's full of them.'

'But they don't all try to take their own lives.'

'It's not your own life,' said Daisy. 'How did you get that idea?'

'I don't think you're meant to talk to me like that. Give me a drink at once. Run out and buy me a morning paper.'

'I go off duty at 7 a.m.,' said Daisy, 'and I have to be in bed at 9 a.m. prompt.'

'Where is your bed, Flo?'

The superintending night nurse, patrolling the wards, approached in time to hear 23 repeating plaintively, 'Where is her bed? And who will get me a morning paper? On whom will that duty fall?'

'You need a clean draw-sheet, Saunders.'

'Yes, Sister.'

They went back down the ward and at the duty desk the Sister asked, 'Delirious?'

'Yes, I think so, Sister. He's excitable, anyway.'

'Temperature 98.2, thirst, vomiting, delirious, restless, that's all that needs to go in the book. If he's excitable, probably not a typhoid state. You may make yourself a cup of cocoatina.'

Only at night were the nurses allowed into the ward kitchen. Like the wards, it was painted dark green up to shoulder height, and above that, cream, with kettles the size of cauldrons. All this was commonplace, but the ward kitchen belonged to the midnight hours, when those who should be sleepers were workers, and the human mind and body sank to their lowest point.

When a constable called round in the morning Matron absolutely refused to let him see James Elder in Alexandra Ward until further notice. This was her usual policy, and the police were used to it. To the constable's alarm, he was sent to Matron's office, to be told that the hospital had been given no address and no satisfactory identification for this patient. The constable offered a report from the station, stating that Elder's underclothes and his letters, all of which were bills, suggested that he was a gentleman.

'Are the motives of gentlemen who jump off Blackfriars Bridge very different from those who are not gentlemen?' asked Matron sharply.

'I can't say,' said the constable, 'they're always at it, Matron, as you know. The Respiration's always on standby. We use the old method, Sylvester's method.' The matron frowned. At this point Dr Sage, without invitation, and apparently with time on his hands, joined the conference. 'Constable,' he said, with intense feeling, 'you've been sent here by your superiors to linger at the bedside of an unfortunate who has attempted what, in this country, is still legally a crime. If, in fact, he had not attempted but succeeded, if this man had drowned himself, would you have proceeded to drag the oozing cadaver into the magistrate's court, and asked for a committal? Would these have been your instructions?' The constable said that the matron hadn't so far given him permission to linger by the bedside at all, but the station would like to be notified if Elder was discharged.

'That is in our hands,' said Dr Sage, holding both his hands aloft, as if to prove they were there. The constable left, saying that in his experience most of these cases made a good recovery if they were kept quiet and given beef-tea.

By the next day, James Elder did not remember saying he lived in Wapping. The envelopes in his pockets had a name, but no address. No friends or connections appeared. There was nothing about him in the newspapers, at any rate nothing was seen by anyone in the hospital who had time to look at them. Matron took the *Morning Post*, the doctors glanced, so they said, at *The Times*, the juniors read the *Daily Mail* and in the hospital kitchen there were copies of *Tit-Bits* and the *Police Gazette* and the local, which came out three times a week. Newspapers were not allowed in the wards.

Dr Sage put 23 on milk and soda, with alcohol and ammonia as a stimulant, and steel drops to guard against anaemia. 'We'll soon see the last of you,' he said in the voice which comforted many. But James Elder refused to eat or drink anything at all, and since his stomach had been empty when he was admitted, he did poorly. – Talk to him, find a good moment, make him see it's all for his own good, persuade him. – Daisy was put on the job: have a go at him, Saunders. Strong, reassuring, smiling, never gives up. He knew her voice, his memory seemed to prick up its ears. You were the one on duty, you were the one that was going to fetch my paper. – Daisy had been instructed to offer a glass of the warm milk, which she did, though inwardly feeling that no-one could gain anyone's confidence with warm milk, on which the skin was just forming. At once she became an enemy who had withheld the newspaper or destroyed it or who was too crass to understand the printed word. 'It said

GALLANT SUICIDE ATTEMPT. Didn't you learn to read in Board School?'

'We're all of us a bit slow in here,' said Daisy. 'You're sick of us nurses, you need some visitors. We could wire them, you know, from the telegraph office.'

He said nothing.

'There was somebody you knew called Flo. Was that Flora, or was she Florence?'

'Bitch.'

'I'm not getting anywhere with my 23,' Daisy told Kate.

'Have you got a smash on him?'

'I've got a smash on the whole ward,' said Daisy. 'It's one of my six half-days on Wednesday. If any of them have the brass to die while I'm out, I'll make them sorry they ever were born.'

Two and a half days later James Elder had still taken nothing by the mouth. He was a screen case, and of great entertainment value to the other patients, who all assumed that because he could not be seen, he would not be able to hear what they said. To all of them, except the dying, food was of paramount interest. The doctor would have to get some kind of food into No. 23 one way or another, frontways, or backways.

Dr Sage, reckless prescriber as he was, was implacably opposed to forced feeding. 'They tell me it's legal to do it to lunatics and to women who want to have the vote. What about it, Sister, what about it, eh, Nurse? A fortnight in the third division, hunger strike, steel gag, choke up chicken? You'll tell me that's got nothing to do with respectable hospital practice. Well, they've thought up all sorts of dodges. In the children's wards I've found them rubbing the little brutes with castor oil in the hope that some of it will sink in and nourish them. But I say a man, a woman, a child, a lunatic, has the right to decide whether to go on living or not. And in all the short chapter, that's to say in all the long chequered story of medical science, show me one man, one woman, one child, one lunatic that doesn't know whether he's hungry or not.'

Matron's opinion, given only to her deputy, was that it was fortunate Dr Sage couldn't be on duty twenty-four hours out of the twenty-four.

Both of them knew that Dr Sage, who had trained as an alienist, was a partner in a mental home somewhere in the country. Believing, as he did, that what is said by children and by the mentally disturbed should be considered just as seriously as any other evidence, he needed a place well away from London to make his own painstaking notes without, so to speak, appearing in character.

'I'm surprised, though, that he's a supporter of women's suffrage,' said the deputy matron.

'He isn't. He doesn't think anyone should have the vote at all.'

Chapter Twelve

KELLY

On Wednesday, her half-day, Daisy, in her cloth coat and large tam o'shanter, walked down to the river. She had known the many voices, not all of them friendly, of the river, ever since she was a child, and missed them now she no longer crossed it twice a day. She allowed herself two minutes only, just enough to watch a barge go past, then went to the Borough Library. The Library was connected with the public wash-house by the municipal fumigation rooms, where books could be disinfected after an outbreak of disease and old clothes could be boiled before redistribution to the needy. The three long low buildings, lettered in white on their grey and red brick, were a powerful image of compulsory cleanliness, inner and outer.

In the crowded reading-room of the library, dozing in the hot metallic breath of the radiator, an old man who seemed almost grown into his seat bent over a pile of the *Blackfriars, Vauxhall and Temple Gazette*.

'Pardon me, but could I just have a look at those locals,' said Daisy. 'I'll give them back to you in a moment.'

'They won't let me sit here if I ain't reading,' he complained.

'If they say anything to you I'll tell them to stow it,' she said, already halfway through the first copy.

'That ain't the way to talk to them, they've got power over you.'

'It's the way I talk to them,' said Daisy.

There were only three pages of news in the paper. The last

issue led off with the Local Government Board's Campaign for the installation of water-closets in city housing, then local weddings, the Oddfellows' annual dinner and glee-singing, and a story (with a photograph) about a kitten which was blown across the room after an explosion, but landed safely in a lady's hat, which had providentially been left on the ground. The story and photograph were said to have been sent to them by a reader.

As a seeker of jobs, Daisy was very well used to small newspaper offices, although she hadn't been in one since she went to put in a paragraph after her mother's death. She had got accustomed to making her way upstairs, across threadbare lino, and through a narrow passage left between piles of old copies waiting for the waste-paper collectors. She opened a frosted glass door and said at once: 'Don't ask me if I want to put in an advertisement. I want to see the editor.'

There were two men in the room, one much older than the other, and an office-boy, who was just taking his coat off the hook. They glanced up as the door opened, and saw that she was good-looking, but not a lady. There was no need for them to get up or to stop smoking. The younger man pushed out a chair for her with his stretched-out foot.

'Sit down, dear, and turn off the hot tap.'

'It's easy for you to talk like that,' said Daisy, sitting down. 'It's not so easy for me. There's something I want to ask you. I ain't got much time.'

The office-boy put on his cap. Like his employers, he was already wearing his coat in the miserably cold office. Collecting a pile of envelopes, he left. So small was the room that his going made a considerable difference, and there was silence for a moment. Daisy began again: 'I want you to print a paragraph, a news paragraph, about a man who tried to commit suicide a few days ago, but he was rescued and brought back to life.' The truth was that she had scarcely considered at all what she was going to say. 'He says his name is James Elder.'

'Anyone can say that,' said the elderly man. 'You'll

probably find he's called Younger.' He sank back into shabby inattention, fidgeting with the paste-pot.

'Well, so James Elder tried to commit suicide,' said the editor. 'Swallowed something, did he?'

'No, he didn't. He threw himself off the Adelphi stairs.'

'And didn't sink. Tut! Tut!'

'He was pulled out. I told you that,' said Daisy. Tired out, she braced herself.

'Are you a relative?' asked the elderly man.

'No, I'm not.'

'Don't give up hope, my dear. If he's still in one piece, he may put it to you yet.'

The editor sat up straight. 'The story's no use to us. There's twenty-one suicides a year off the steps, and our readers aren't interested in drowned men, only drowned women. There's no local interest.'

'Yes, there is,' said Daisy. 'He's in the Blackfriars. He won't eat, he's letting himself die there.'

'Does he talk?'

'Not much.'

The editor rocked to and fro on his chair, letting it balance for a while on only one leg. Then he said: 'I'm Thomas Kelly.' The elderly man muttered, 'I'm Sweedon.'

'I am Daisy Saunders.'

'What's your game, Daisy?'

'I haven't got one,' she cried. 'I've brought you a story for your paper, a better one than all that about hats and kittens, if you weren't too thick to see it.'

'We get quite a lot of items from the Blackfriars,' said Kelly. 'If anything happens in the hospital, say the doctors cut off a couple of legs too many, I've got someone there who gives us a word in time. I've heard nothing about James Elder, though. What I want to know is, how did you?'

'What difference does that make?'

'You're still sure you're not a relation?'

'No, I don't hardly know him!'

'What good would it do you, then, if we did print it?'

Daisy answered carefully. 'Well, it might do him some good. He's not quite in his right mind. I think it's the only thing that interests him. And so – '

'You're a nurse at the Blackfriars, aren't you?'

'No, I'm not,' said Daisy. 'Do I look like a nurse?'

'Yes, you do, as a matter of fact,' said Kelly.

Daisy sat still, with her hands folded in her lap.

'What I said was true. I'm not a nurse, yet, I'm a second-year probationer.'

'It's all the same. You're nursing this joker, aren't you? You're supposed to treat the confidential details of your cases as sacred, and on no account to divulge them, except in a court of law.'

'You aren't going to put it in about him, then,' said Daisy. 'I've asked you straight, and you won't put it in.'

'I never said I would or I wouldn't,' said Kelly, tapping his teeth with a pencil. 'What are you going to do next?'

'I'll go and see another editor,' said Daisy, getting to her feet. 'You're ten a penny the other side of the river. There's plenty of weeklies in south London.'

'You're in trouble,' said Kelly. 'You weren't very sensible to come here.' She hadn't been asked, when she first came in, to take off her coat, and that was a godsend when it came to getting out of the place. On the staircase she passed the office boy coming back from the post. They could barely squeeze past each other. The boy looked at her, and asked her if she felt all right. She said that she did.

In 1911 the Aerated Bread Company provided a Ladies' Room on the first floor of their tea-shops. It was one of London's first acknowledgements of the fact that there were now a multitude of women workers who wanted to sit down in peace and spend the money which they had earned, if only on a piece of toast. If there wasn't time for the ABC you had to go to a tea-and-coffee stall, and Daisy stopped at one she knew pretty well, near the car park in the next street but one. As she took out her purse to find the money, someone moved up behind her and put a penny down on the stall's counter to pay for her before she had time to do it. His penny was underneath her penny. It was the editor of the *Blackfriars, Vauxhall and Temple Gazette*. Standing there in the dingy vanity of his billycock hat and checked suit he said: 'You're going the wrong way for Southwark.'

'I'm not going there,' she said. 'You know that.'

'I'll walk along with you a bit. I'm not sure that you saw me at my best in the office.'

'I don't know what your best is,' said Daisy. 'Is that why you went and came after me?'

'Something riled me,' he admitted. 'We don't often get a young woman in by herself.'

'Have you left that poor Mr Sweedon to do the lot, then?'

'There's not all that much to do, just the pasting up. Two to one he's gone out for a wet. I'd sack him if I wasn't a generous soul.'

'Does that paper belong to you, then?'

'Give her another tea,' Kelly told the stallholder. – 'No, it's owned by the printers.'

'Then they're the generous souls,' said Daisy. 'I don't want any more, thanks.'

They were walking together across the Blackfriars Bridge, where the din of the horse-traffic was louder than the motorbuses. 'You're irritating me,' Kelly persisted. 'All I asked you was what you thought of me.'

'I'd like you to tell me something first. When I came in, why couldn't you give me a straight answer to a straight question?'

'It's a habit I've got into,' said Kelly, 'and I felt it would be a kindness to you to put you in your place.'

'Well, all I thought was: I'm sorry for that man, if he's like that now, what'll he be in ten years' time?'

'Ten years' time, I can tell you that,' Kelly said sourly. 'I'll be dead.'

'What makes you think that? You look well enough.'

'I'll have to go and be shot, though, if the cousins don't stop quarrelling. I'm a Territorial.' She stared at him. 'Didn't you know the King had a German cousin?'

'I don't read the papers much,' said Daisy.

He had her by the elbow. A passer-by might have taken them for friends. 'Don't hold me so tight,' said Daisy. 'I bruise easy.' She stopped at a point where a sooty building was divided from the pavement by iron railings and a few feet of stone flags covered with bird droppings. 'I'm going in here,' she said.

'You can't go in there, that's a church!'

'Well, I'm going in there.'

'Whatever for?' he cried out. 'If you want to get rid of me, surely there's easier ways of doing it.'

'What's wrong with going into a church?' asked Daisy.

'You can't believe all that,' Kelly shouted in real distress. 'All that's made up to keep you quiet, and they collect your money on top of it. A smart girl like you, a nurse, that knows what's what, you can't believe there's a God up there keeping a list of everything you do. You can't believe there was a Jesus who went about turning loaves into fishes.' He took off his hat, put his cigarette behind his ear and followed her through the main door and the green baize doors set at a right-angle inside. The candles had been lit for evensong. 'Nothing they do in here is of any perishing use,' said Kelly in a hoarse whisper. 'I don't give a Friar Tuck for anything they do in here.'

'You don't have to whisper,' said Daisy. 'Just talk quiet.'

A sacristan came out of the vestry and opened a door in one of the pillars, an imitation, built in 1876, of the columns of San Miniato. There was a cupboard inside from which he took a broom, a dustpan and a brush, and began to sweep up the nave.

'That's the kind of thing I mean!' Kelly cried angrily, and then turned on her. 'You're not religious anyway. You're a liar.'

Chapter Thirteen

DAISY LEAVES LONDON

When Daisy got back to the hospital (she was on duty at six) she found that the screens had been taken away from No. 23 in Alexandra Ward. During the afternoon James Elder had been discharged. A middle-aged woman, giving the name of Floreen Harris, had called round, spoken to the medical officer on duty and the secretary, signed the necessary papers and taken Elder away in a cab.

The day after next, a Friday, the *Blackfriars, Vauxhall and Temple Gazette* printed a headline on its local news page: MYSTERY OF 'MINISTERING ANGEL'. The paragraph beneath it spoke of James Elder, of no known address, at present lying at the point of death in the Blackfriars Hospital. His story had been related exclusively to the *Gazette* by a charming informant, whose interest in the unfortunate man had been evident in spite of her attempts to conceal her agitation, giving rise to the suspicion that she was a member of the nursing staff at the hospital. Throughout the interview, the paragraph continued, she had remained closely veiled.

When Daisy was sent for to Matron's office the *Gazette* was lying open on the desk, so that she could read, upside down, MYSTERY OF 'MINISTERING ANGEL'. When Matron turned the paper round, she was able, at sickening speed, to read the rest of the paragraph.

'Well, Saunders?'

'I never thought he'd do that!'

'I don't quite follow you. You don't deny that you gave

information about a patient – one for whom you had a special responsibility, but that is not the point at issue – you gave information about him to a newspaper. Now you tell me that you didn't expect it to be printed.'

'I did at first. Then I didn't. I went to the office. I wasn't closely veiled, I hadn't a veil on at all.'

'Why did you go there, Saunders?'

'I thought it would be of benefit to the patient if he could see something about himself in the paper.'

'You thought you were carrying out the doctor's orders?'

'No, Matron.'

'Did he give you special instructions of this kind?'

'No, Matron, he didn't.'

'You have been trained at this hospital for nearly two years to think, but not to think that you know best. You were doing, from all reports, very well. However, your training has failed. Why was that?'

It was made clear that she must leave by Monday week. This was a concession, because it was known that Daisy had no home to go to. Kate Smith and some of the eighteen other second-year probationers – but not all of them, some were cautious – bought a leaving present for her. There was not much time, and they had to settle for a travelling salt-and-pepper set, said to be new china, and decorated with a view of the coronation of George V. Daisy was grateful. Disgrace contaminates, even though it makes everyone else feel a little safer.

When she went to hand back her uniform and apron to stores, she was told that someone from the kitchens wanted to see her before she left.

It was a dark little woman, bundled into a sacking apron. 'You remember me. I am Mrs Martinez. They don't let me be a nurse. I took employment here in the kitchens.'

'How is the baby, Mrs Martinez?'

'Always asking for you.' This seemed unlikely. 'I still have your two shilling. I didn't ask you for it because I was poor. I asked because you never forget anyone who borrows money from you and I don't want you to forget me.'

'I'd sooner everyone forgot me,' said Daisy, kissing Mrs Martinez, who asked where she was going.

'I'm going to Cambridge. It's not much of a chance, but I can't think of anything else to do. Dr Sage has a private hospital quite near Cambridge. He's there when he's not here, that's Wednesday and Saturdays. I got his address from Admissions. I am going to take a day return to Cambridge and ask if he'll see me.'

'Oh, but he is very mad,' said Mrs Martinez. 'One day he flung the beef-tea.'

'You go back to the kitchen, my dear. Don't get caught on this floor.'

'You know best,' said Mrs Martinez.

The best way to go to Cambridge was from King's Cross. Daisy went from Liverpool Street, which worked out cheaper. She had hardly ever been out of London. She and her mother never went to see the house at Hastings – all that was left to the solicitor, although if she'd been nineteen then, as she very nearly was now, she would have acted different. Twice she'd been on a school outing to the seaside. Once, at Southend, they'd stayed late, and gone out on the water in boats with Japanese lanterns. The lights and the colours, brilliant yellow and red, were reflected in the dark slap and wash of the sea. The Boys' Brigade played from the shore. The music travelled across the water as though it was going to settle there.

As she went to buy her ticket in soot-blackened Liverpool Street station she thought, suppose it happens again. The old trick, the old game. Never look back. Someone touched her, and a hand covered her half-crown with another half-crown. 'Lord, it can't be Kelly again,' she said, still not turning round. 'You've fooled yourself this time. I'm going out of town.'

'I know you are,' said Kelly. 'You're going to Cambridge. I told you I had someone in the kitchens at the Blackfriars who tipped me the wink.'

'I don't think you mentioned the kitchens,' said Daisy. She took her ticket and turned away. 'I suppose there's someone who wants to earn a bit extra there, like all the rest of us.'

'I'm coming with you to Cambridge,' said Kelly, walking after her, heel and toe, like a music-hall comic. 'Do you know the town well?'

'I don't know it at all,' said Daisy.

'Well, I'll watch out and see as you come to no harm.'

'That's the reason, is it?'

Liverpool Street was still lit by gas, and in the greenish light Kelly looked seedy and worn at the edges – how old was he? – but he felt the obligation to be jaunty still.

'No, I'm coming because I'm eaten up with remorse at putting you out of a job. I didn't write that piece, by the way, Sweedon did.'

'Is that true?'

'No, Sweedon can't write anything. He can't hardly write his own pawn-tickets. I wrote it – had style, didn't it? Where's your box?'

'It's in the Left Luggage. If Dr Sage gives me a berth, I shall tell the railway to send it on. Stand out of my way now, Kelly, my train's going in five minutes.'

'Women always think the train's going in five minutes. Trains start according to the time-table.'

Daisy looked him up and down.

He added, not at all as if he had never said it before, 'I know a hotel in Cambridge, quite near the station.'

'Where they don't ask questions, and if they did, they'd ask me, "What can you be thinking of coming here with that little runt?"'

Kelly looked stung. Then he recovered and said: 'It'll be your first time, won't it?' – Daisy said, 'I suppose when I came to the office like that you thought I looked easy.' – Kelly said,

'I thought you were in an awkward fix. I wasn't surprised that
a hospital nurse should be after the patients. What else do
they go into it for? But I thought you must be more than
ordinary fond of men if you was going to risk losing your job on
account of this James Elder.' – 'I didn't mean to lose it,' said
Daisy. 'I love nursing.' – 'You need a man, though,' said
Kelly. 'I mean a man of some kind. That's what I am, dearie,
a man of some kind. I'll look after you, Daisy Saunders. I
won't marry you, that's not my style, apart from being
married already, but I'll look after you, I give you my dicky-
bird.' – 'You mean you'll pay for one night at a hotel that don't
ask no questions,' said Daisy, whose eyes were full of tears.

'Two nights, Daisy, three nights. You want to get used to it.
What else can you do? I can't see there's anyone else wants
you. I want you, though, Daisy Saunders. It's nothing. You
just want to take a couple of whiskies.'

'I don't drink,' said Daisy.

'Is that true?'

'No,' Daisy answered. 'I never had a whisky, though.'

She felt pity for them both.

'You'd better come, I suppose,' she said. 'I don't expect you
know Cambridge any better than I do, but I don't see as I can
stop you.'

He put his arm round her waist, fingering her. What a pair
we make, she thought. He doesn't deserve any better, no more
do I.

Part Three

Chapter Fourteen

NO MYSTERY ABOUT DAISY'S MOVEMENTS

Fred put the two sheets of writing paper with a small collection of other unposted beginnings of letters to Dear Miss Saunders which he couldn't bring himself to throw away from a conviction, – something stronger, anyway, than a superstition – that was quite at odds with his rational self. This conviction was that if he destroyed his earlier efforts he would destroy, at the same time, his chance of finishing one at all. Yet the contents of the letters were already decided. He could have finished the first one, he could have finished any of them at any time. After seeing Daisy at close quarters for let us say half an hour – though perhaps with not very clear vision – and having, he thought, addressed nine remarks to her and had eight answers – those he could still repeat word for word – he knew that he must marry her. There was, from that point of view, nothing more to say.

It must be spoken about as soon as possible to Professor Flowerdew. The Professor hadn't expressed any sympathy or indeed made any comment about Fred's accident, because he had never heard anything about it. He had been in Vienna, and had missed the first few days of term. He knew nothing of his young assistant's fall. He was, however, in a state of distress. This, Fred knew, had been caused by the growing invasion of physics by the pernicious notion of mass. The conservation of mass, it seemed, was to be taken as a principle, along with the constancy of matter. But Flowerdew didn't believe that mass was indestructible, or matter either, and where, he asked, was mass anyway? A crude notion of substance was slipping (or being slipped) unnoticed into science, proving itself constantly insufficient, and always under the necessity of being reduced to smaller and smaller particles. And once again the professor urged upon Fred that to base one's calculations on unobservables – such as God, such as the soul, such as the atom, such as the elementary particle – was nothing more than a comforting weakness. 'I don't deny that all human beings need comfort. But scientists should not indulge themselves on quite this scale.'

At the same time Flowerdew reproached himself because his assistant had not yet started upon his own programme of research, or even settled what it was to be. It was scarcely the moment, then, for Fred to tell him that it would be necessary, for reasons which were at the same time physical and spiritual, for him to resign his appointment at Angels.

I cannot live without Daisy, Fred thought. There is no God, no spiritual authority, no design, there are no causes and no effects – there is no purpose in the universe, but if there were, it could be shown that there was an intention, throughout recorded and unrecorded time, to give me Daisy.

A week later, (the week during which he had debated at the Disobligers' Society), the porter told Fred that a Mr Wrayburn was in the house and wanted to see him. Fred found Wrayburn in the normal costume of a scholar off duty – tweed knickerbockers and a stiff collar – but agitated, and trembling a little. The work which he did for Dr Matthews – providing occasional notes on the notes on the supplementary and possibly forged manuscripts of the apocalyptic gospels – must, of course, be taxing.

'It's a somewhat delicate matter, Fairly.'

Wrayburn seemed to want to go neither in nor out, so, as there was no-one for the moment in the court, the two of them began to walk round the walnut tree.

'Well, perhaps "delicate" is not the right word,' said Wrayburn. 'I'm hardly a judge of whether it's delicate or not.'

He fell silent, so Fred said, 'Is it to do with Dr Matthews?'

Immediately, like a slot-machine, Wrayburn wheezed and clattered into a stream of words. 'It has nothing whatever to do with Dr Matthews, and even if I felt tempted to do so, you can hardly imagine that I should confide in someone so much younger than myself, a mere acquaintance, and a man who knows nothing, and less than nothing, about palaeography. I do, however, want to say that because of the minute nature of my work, necessitating long stretches of concentration, I am perhaps more easily surprised, and more easily upset, than most people. I'm not talking, Fairly, about your accident of ten days ago. But yes, I admit, this has been a surprise to me.'

'What has?' asked Fred. 'What's happened?'

'I don't say that it was impossibly late, I suppose it may have been about a quarter or twenty past nine. She was the only person I ever remember arriving at our house on a laundry-van. It appears that she asked for a lift at the station. But then, there had been no suggestion of her coming back at all.'

'Has Miss Saunders come back?' Fred asked, his heart dilated and closed as though what he felt was fear.

'Yes, I thought I made that clear.'

'You didn't make it clear, you cretin. Why didn't you tell me at once?'

'Fairly, are you out of your senses?'

Fred recollected himself. 'Was I speaking loudly?'

'Yes, very.'

'Perhaps you could tell me what Miss Saunders said.'

'Your voice was threatening, Fairly.'

'Perhaps you could tell me what she said, and what she's doing here. She must have asked for me, as you very kindly took the trouble to come round to the college.'

'Not at all, she hasn't asked for you at all. Venetia, too, thought that you ought not to be approached over the matter. But I exercised my own judgement. I don't want any further burden of housekeeping on her shoulders. Ever since we moved out of Cambridge there have been difficulties over domestic staff, though speaking for myself I don't see that you could find an easier household to work for. All I require – '

'Is Daisy staying in your house? Is she at Guestingley Road? For God's sake, Wrayburn, if you can't tell me anything else, tell me that.'

Wrayburn said coldly that he believed his wife had accommodated Miss Saunders in one of the attics. 'You can't expect me to occupy myself with such matters.'

'I don't expect it. You came here because you didn't want your wife to have to be responsible for her. Of course you didn't. Of course she mustn't be. But for God's sake have the sense not to let Daisy slip. Don't let her get back to London again. Lock the doors. Talk to her quietly and seriously. Knock her on the head, give her a sleeping draught.'

'You're distraught, Fairly. You gave me to understand that you had no connection with this young woman.'

They could not expect to walk much longer by themselves round the great walnut tree. The Treasurer, side by side with the Master, was coming out from the next door. Supporting himself on the Treasurer's arm, the Master with an agile movement, stretched down to put first one palm, then the back of his hand on the grass.

'It will rain on Wednesday,' he said. 'Who was it wanted to know?'

During the reverse process the Master, never losing his dignity, gently raised himself back to the upright. Fred followed Wrayburn out and caught up with him bicycling north-westward. 'I haven't any connection with her,' he called out. 'Can't you see that's the trouble?'

In fact there was no mystery about Daisy's movements. Mystery is a luxury and would have been quite beyond her means. She had come back to Cambridge because she could not think of anyone who was likely to take her on, except Dr Sage. To be more accurate, she did not know anyone who had a private hospital except Dr Sage. She had come to the Wrayburns because she had nowhere else to go. She said nothing about where she had been during the intervening days. With the fare back from London, and a shilling to the driver of the laundry van, she had come to the end of her money, but she did not intend to ask for something for nothing.

When Mrs Wrayburn took her up to the attic she saw at once that these were supposed to be the servants' rooms and that there were no servants sleeping in them. Here she was in the room where she had been put to bed with Fred Fairly. She undressed, hung up her skirt, and washed under the cold-water tap on the landing. The basin was surrounded with sage-green tiles, representing the story of Pelléas and Mélisande. From the attic, if she leaned out, she could just see the lighted windows of the farm from which the cart had come, and the road with a few moving lights going along it, sometimes the bright acetylene headlamps of a motor-car.

In the morning she came downstairs and found Mrs Wrayburn in a distracted condition. 'Daisy – may one call you that? – I must tell you that I've decided recently that as a matter of principle we should live more simply. Fruit, vegetables, a minimum of tea or coffee, since science has proved these to be noxious. Now, as to main dishes, this is a tin which I bought at the new Eustace Miles Emporium in King's Parade. You can read about it on the label, it's all printed there and it's worth knowing for its own sake, particularly if – well, as you can see, this tin contains Health Plasmon, which may be combined with a variety of substances to make nourishing dishes without the necessity of cooking them.'

'It looks like cornflour to me,' said Daisy.

'I think one might get used to it,' said Mrs Wrayburn, trying for a decisive tone. 'I believe in the power of the mind over the body. Yes, I do believe in that. One can get used to anything. Even men can get used to anything.'

'I hope you won't mind if I say this, Mrs Wrayburn,' said Daisy, 'but I don't think your husband's ever going to get used to this stuff, particularly if he has to have it raw. And it's a big house you've got here, with a lot of work needed, and there doesn't seem to be anyone living in.'

'Ah, the empty bedrooms!' said Mrs Wrayburn. 'They should be full of smiling faces and strong, willing hands.'

'You live a bit too far out, I think, Mrs Wrayburn. I shouldn't think you'd get a girl to stay, and if she did there's nowhere to go in the evening except that farm.'

'No, they don't stay for long,' said Mrs Wrayburn. 'No, not for long.' She added, as though one thing followed from the other. 'I studied for four years at Newnham. I was the Organising Secretary of the debating society. I was both the Treasurer and the Organising Secretary of the Women's Social and Political Union.'

She looked at the sink, loaded down with all that was necessary when a husband had his daily meals in the house. Like most of her friends, she had prayed not to marry a clergyman, a general practitioner, or a university lecturer without a fellowship. All these (unlike the Army or the Bar) were professions that meant luncheon at home, so that every day (in addition to cups, plates and dishes) demanded toast-racks, egg-cups, egg-cosies, hot water jugs, hot milk strainers, tea-strainers, coffee-strainers, bone egg-spoons, sugar-tongs, mustard-pots manufactured of blue glass inside, metal out-side, silver fruit knives (as steel in contact with fruit-juice was known to be poisonous), napkins with differently coloured rings for each person at table, vegetable dishes with handles in the shape of artichokes, gravy boats, dishcovers, fish-forks with which it was difficult to eat fish (but fish-knives were only for vulgarians), muffin-dishes which had to be filled with boiling water to keep the muffins at their correct temperature, soup-plates into which the soup was poured from an earthen-ware container with a lid, cut-glass blancmange dishes, knife-rests for knives, fork-rests for forks, cheese dishes with lids the shape of a piece of cheese, compotiers, ramekins, pipkins, cruets, pots. All of these were not too much (on a clean cloth, too, with the centre fold forming a straight line the whole length of the table) for Mr Wrayburn to expect – Mrs Wrayburn did not think it unreasonable, and nor did Daisy – and most of them were in the sink at the moment, waiting, in mute reproach, to be washed and dried.

Daisy and Mrs Wrayburn understood each other at once, and, only a few minutes later, admitted to each other that they did so. Daisy would stay. The room in the attic would be hers. In her spare time she would do the work of the house.

Chapter Fifteen

A WALK IN THE COUNTRY

Wrayburn regretted his hospitality on the night of the accident. Now he saw that he had made a second serious error in telling Fairly about the return of this never quite explained young woman. Fortunately, there was no telephone in his house, but Fairly might plague him by hanging about the place, or even by reappearing in the attics. However, all that Fred did, though admittedly he did it at once, was to send a note asking Miss Saunders if she would come out with him on her day off.

'I suppose if she had been of a different class you would have suggested a chaperone,' he said to his wife. 'I mean, I don't suppose Fairly would allow his own sisters – '

'Oh, my dear, I don't know whether he has any sisters,' said Mrs Wrayburn, 'and I am not in charge of Daisy Saunders. I am not even employing her, or not exactly. I believe I shall become rather fond of her, but I am not in charge.'

'Who is in charge of her then?' Mrs Wrayburn only knew that Dr Sage had taken her on at his mental hospital, and her hours were half-past eight to half-past six.

Fred had asked Daisy whether in spite of their short acquaintance he might call her Daisy, and whether she would like to come out for a walk, a walk in the country. She said it would be the very thing. What about (Fred asked) taking the train to Whittlesford and walking from there to the mill at Great Chishill, only they wouldn't, probably, get so far. Daisy said she was game.

In her thick boots and a flat golfing-cap, which she had found in a trunk in the Wrayburns' attics, she appeared ready for anything. She had turned up the hem of her skirt an inch all the way round. Her colour was higher than usual with excitement as they got out at the station. 'What's this place like?' she asked.

'I don't know. I've been here before but I've never really thought about it.' He looked at her anxiously. 'Ought I to have done? We shall have to head south-west, you know, out of the village.'

'Look!' she said, 'there's a house for sale.'

'What about it, Daisy?'

'Let's go and see round it,' said Daisy, 'we've plenty of time. It cheers you up having a look round an empty house.'

Fred tried to envisage this.

'It's just like shopping,' she explained. 'You don't have to buy anything, it's just to turn the things over.'

'We'd have to go back to Cambridge, I expect, to get the keys,' said Fred, but the keys were only a few doors down the street, according to the card in the window: enquiries at the ironmonger's. The ironmonger began to say that he couldn't spare anyone from the shop to show them round, but lost heart and entrusted the keys to Daisy.

'We won't be long,' she said. 'We're going for a walk in the country.'

The house, like all houses which have stood vacant for any length of time, seemed full of bits of paper. Leaflets, notices of church-services and parish fêtes, circulars, advertisements for auctions, warnings of potato blight, had continued to come and probably were still coming through the cramped letter-box, and blown with the draught about the stone floor were torn-up scraps of bills and fragments of letters in black, blue and violet ink. ' . . . cannot see my way to' . . . 'sday without fail' . . . 'lean on His mercy'. 'I could read these all day, if I wasn't going anywhere else,' she said. 'I don't get a lot of letters, perhaps that's why.'

'People are rather given to sending notes in Cambridge,' said Fred. 'Sometimes I wish they wouldn't. I suppose I get a good many letters. I hope they won't end up like this, torn up on the floor of an empty house.'

Daisy was looking through the drawers. One plate, no knife, one fork, one spoon. 'All by himself, I suppose, you have to be sorry for him.'

'It might have been a woman,' Fred suggested.

'No, you'd never get a woman to live like this. She must have died before he did, or left him.'

'You'd have thought they'd have cleared the place out properly,' said Fred, 'whatever happened.'

'Whoever saw a house cleared out properly?' said Daisy. 'There's always something left.'

The kitchen had a deep stone sink partly full of green moss, although the gaunt old tap could not have dripped for months.

Daisy looked rapidly through the cupboards: nothing there but more scraps of paper and a set of chimney sweep's brushes. One of the floorboards was loose. Probably all the joists were rotten, Fred thought. 'There's something underneath, I expect,' said Daisy. 'Where else had he got to keep anything? All these old men are the same. There's money there, most likely.'

But she would not let Fred lift the board, considering it unlucky. Upstairs – the stairs opened out of one of the cupboards – there was a dark garret, without furniture. No basin, he must have washed in the sink or under one pump, and used the earth closet in the yard, now boarded up, and sinking by slow degrees back into its native soil. Daisy was radiant. She had seen everything, and even knew the name of the one-time owner, having made it out from two of the torn-up envelopes.

They walked back together down the street. It would have been quite different, Fred pointed out, if he had really been looking for a house. But that would ruin it, Daisy told him. He would be worrying about the money, the drains, the size of the rooms, there'd be no go in it. Fred sighed. Was it one of the differences between men and women, that women like to live on their imagination? It's all they can afford, most of them, said Daisy.

'I don't think that ironmonger was took in,' said Daisy, as they got over the stile. 'He knew we'd no intention of buying. He could see how the land lay.'

'How does it lie, Daisy?'

'Well, this is the second time we've ever met. We don't hardly know each other and we aren't anything to each other.'

Fred was appalled. 'Don't you know what you are to me?' he asked.

Daisy considered. 'I suppose I do know, Fred. To tell you the truth, a child of six would notice it.'

'But that's just what I want. I want children of six to notice it, I want ironmongers to notice it.'

'Fred, you've got a family, haven't you?'

Fred explained that his father was Rector of Blow, and also what a rector was, as distinguished from a vicar. He admitted to a mother and two sisters, and said that he wanted every one of them to notice that he was in love.

'Fred, quite honestly, did you ever take a girl out before?'

He seemed to find this difficult, but only for a few moments. 'I've never taken out a girl I wanted to marry before.'

'She mayn't have known that, though,' said Daisy.

'Why should they matter, Daisy? Why, even if they existed, should they matter? They don't exist and didn't exist. They're unobservables.'

Daisy quarrelled much less than most people with time. The past did not occupy her thoughts unless it had to, nor did the future. At the present moment she was on a country walk, and she wanted to do things right. In particular, she was prepared to be impressed by quantities of birds and flowers.

The first meadow was flooded to about an inch deep, and lay under water as though under silvery glass, with the long grasses flattened and lying together under the slight current that rippled across them. The stream was too high to cross by the little bridge, they had to skirt round the top edge of the meadow. Once they were on higher ground it was as awkward as a walk across fields usually is, the path having been made by farm carts, so that you had to choose whether to stay on the high ridge in the centre or on one of the broad muddy ruts on each side. In Fred's judgement, Daisy was entitled to the dry but higher ground, but walking there she was almost at the same height as himself. When she jumped down beside him they hardly had room to walk side by side. The only way possible was to go arm in arm.

What about the birds, what about the wild flowers? Fred felt with keen anxiety that since Daisy had mentioned them he ought to be able to produce at least some of them. The whole sweep of the pale green hedgeless fields seemed empty, except for some distant cattle which had just been turned out. The spring wheat hardly showed. It was as different as possible from the country round Blow, so much less rich, less watched, less beautiful, less sinister. Here the sky stretched to a horizon without event, almost without landmark, so that a church looked only a mile away when in fact it was four or five. In the last five years Fred had got used to these shining fields. The first long walk he had taken in this direction had been with Professor Flowerdew and a lecturer in moral philosophy from King's, who had said, as they tramped up this very same cart track, Flowerdew, I am finally convinced that the physical and the psychical are two different aspects of the same reality – Absurd! the Professor had called back over his shoulder. This field is not an aspect of anything. It is a field. My mind is not an aspect of anything, it is a mind and only differs from the field because it directs its own activity.

'What were those birds?' Daisy asked. 'Were they quails, Fred?'

'No, I'm afraid not, I'm afraid they were fieldfares.'

'That's a pity,' said Daisy. 'I should like to have seen a quail.'

About flowers, Fred knew much less, leaving them, on the whole, to his sisters. He had hoped for early primroses, but there were none. Daisy, however, found in the grass by one side of the path, a number of tiny, whitish-and-greenish, insignificant looking flowers, not the same as each other, which he thought must be mouse-ears or chickweeds.

'This one's different, though,' she said. 'That's a throatwort. You have to be careful, though, if you're thinking of making a medicine out of it. It could make things worse.'

She had taken off her gloves and was holding the miserable little plant delicately in her strong fingers.

'Look, five petals. You can count them.'

'They've all got five petals,' said Fred. 'I should never have known the difference.' He looked at it with respect. 'Is that really called throatwort?'

'No, of course it isn't,' said Daisy. 'I don't know what it is. I don't know what any of them are. I only said it to keep things going.'

She could see that he was troubled. 'You must always tell me the truth. I'm lost if I can't depend on you,' he said.

They walked on.

'They did depend on me at the Blackfriars. I am a good nurse. That's not just vanity. Matron said I was the sort of nurse she wanted. Particularly with the post-operationals, and if she said that, she meant it, you can bet your Jimmy Skinner.'

'Why did you leave London, then? Did you get tired of it?'

'I wouldn't ever get tired of it,' she said. 'But there's a rule, you know, that you mustn't discuss the patients' cases, not outside the hospital, that is.'

'And you did?'

'Yes, I did.'

'Why, Daisy?'

'I thought I'd help him to get what he wanted. I thought really it would help to save his life.'

'And it did?'

'No, it didn't.'

'Did he die?'

'No, but his life didn't need saving.'

A little later they sat down for a rest, which neither of them particularly needed, in the graveyard of a flint and pebble church. Although there was an old pumping mill a hundred yards away, a number of the tombstones belonged to men, women and children drowned in the floods. The sun at last could be felt as warmth and Daisy took off the golfing cap, into which she had stuck her white-flowered plant. The cap smelt of camphor.

'I think the sun's bringing it out worse. It was in one of the clothes chests upstairs and Mrs Wrayburn said I could borrow it.'

'I can't imagine Mrs Wrayburn playing golf,' said Fred. 'There's no reason why she shouldn't, but I just can't picture it.'

'She told me it belonged to her brother. She kept it when he went to Rangoon.'

'My sisters love me,' Fred told her. 'Or anyway the younger one does. But I don't believe that if I went to Rangoon either of them would keep any of my things a day longer than necessary.'

'Perhaps she wishes she was a child again,' Daisy suggested. 'She might feel she'd taken a wrong turning in life.'

'Don't put it on again,' said Fred.

They would never get to Great Chishill, but they agreed that they didn't expect to. Daisy admitted that she was thirsty. Without landmarks, the broad fields deceived and Fred felt that he was risking his whole reputation by saying that a double line of willows ahead of them, raised a few feet, was a side road and that they would find a public house there, The Fenny Inn. They walked on, and it was a road, and there was The Fenny Inn, looking as though it had been fished out of the marshy water, rather than built with hands, but still, indisputably, a public house.

'Have you ever been in there?' Daisy asked.

'No, I've only passed by it, but if you don't like it we'll walk out of it immediately.'

'Where would we go to?'

'I don't know, but if you don't like it we'll walk out of it immediately.'

Evidently he meant it and Daisy perceived at that moment that what he was offering her was the best of himself, keeping nothing back, the best, then, that one human being can offer to another.

They went into the unwelcoming bar, lit by one window, high up and hazy with damp. Pike and eels might have swum past it, the whole room might have been beneath the fens.

'I've never been anywhere nicer,' said Daisy.

'Are you sure?'

'No, but I was afraid we were going to walk out immediately.'

'I don't know why you laugh at me all the time,' said Fred. 'I'm in deadly earnest.'

Daisy sat down and stretched herself luxuriously inch by inch against the hard back of the settle. What would she like? Half a pint of milk stout, but The Fenny Inn couldn't supply that, so half a pint of Cambridge Ale.

'It's very nice,' she said.

'But it's not what you asked for.'

Daisy sipped and talked. 'You know the nurses did a bit of dram drinking at the hospital, at least the older ones did. It was the backache when you were coming off the wards, you couldn't blame them. It was like a saw. They just kept a lump of sugar ready and then they kept the gin in a surgical spirit bottle. Gin is surgical spirit, really.'

'Daisy, will you marry me?'

She looked down at her glass.

'I know you don't say what you don't mean, Fred.'

'Will you think about it?'

Daisy would have given the world to tell him, down to the bottom, what she truly felt. All her life she had been at a great disadvantage in finding it so much more easy to give than to take. Hating to see anyone in want, she would part without a thought with money or possessions, but she could accept only with the caution of a half-tamed animal.

'I don't say I won't, Fred.'

Chapter Sixteen

A VISIT FROM THE FAIRLYS

Mr Wrayburn took alarm. For something which was as good as going on under his own roof he might, in retrospect, be blamed. His wife told him that it was absurd that he should have put himself out in any way, and that as far as his own roof was concerned, Fred, except on the first occasion, had never come any farther than the hall. He had taken Daisy out, and brought her back. Subsequently he had invited Herbert himself to dine at Angels, where they had had some odd music and some very good Madeira, 'according to your own account, Herbert.' Where could any blame lie? Mr Wrayburn did not explain, but said that he believed Fairly came of quite decent people.

A word to Daisy might, perhaps, be all that was necessary. But he had never spoken to her before at any length. How to begin? She didn't (Venetia told him) come back from the mental hospital until after seven. Then she went straight to the kitchen, where he knew he did best not to set foot. But there was no help for it, so he stood there while Daisy sorted out the washing. Every now and again his own shirts and undergarments passed before his eyes.

'Miss Saunders, have you ever happened to hear Verdi's opera, *La Traviata*?'

'I know a song out of that,' said Daisy. 'It's in my Vocal Gems selection.'

'In *La Traviata* the hero, a simple, honourable young man of good family, becomes obsessed with Violetta, a woman of light reputation. Don't, please, think that I am pressing the comparison. However, the hero's father arrives in Paris and pleads with him to go back to old Provence, where, as a matter of fact, he came from in the first place.'

'Why is it "old" Provence?' asked Daisy.

'The son at first refuses. Perhaps you'll wonder why I'm telling you all this.'

'I'm not wondering at all,' said Daisy. 'You'll think I'm too thick to understand if you say what you mean straight out.'

'The father, you see, is distressed because he fears that if his son cannot be separated from the Traviata, his life and career will be, to all intents and purposes, ruined. He explains this to Violetta.'

Daisy had intended her last remark to silence Mr Wrayburn, but she had a weakness for a good story. 'Well, what happens next?'

Wrayburn floundered. 'In the sense that you mean, nothing happens. The problem solves itself. Violetta dies of consumption.'

'We don't call it that now,' said Daisy. 'But anyway, what does she have to say about it?'

'She says, I want to live.' Wrayburn searched his memory. 'The old father regrets his harshness, but that is scarcely the point.'

'You want to tell me that I am no good for Fred,' said Daisy calmly. 'But I'm quite healthy, I never heard of anything like that in my family.'

'You've quite misunderstood me. I mean that if Fairly marries you, or indeed any other young woman, he will have to give up his position as Junior Fellow of his college. That was a condition of his taking up the appointment, as he must very well have known. There are no married fellows at St Angelicus. In addition, no woman is allowed to set foot in the college. The Master and Fellows, in short, are celibates.'

'So are Father Haggett and the Curate at the church I used to go to,' said Daisy. 'But there's women round at the Presbytery all day and half the night asking him for something or other.'

'Miss Saunders, I don't want you to be disappointed by what I have been saying. It was, in a sense, my duty to speak to you.'

'In what sense?' Daisy asked. 'Fred could have told me himself if he'd wanted to.'

'He is very unlikely to want to. That is my drift.'

Fred took her to *Cox and Box*, given by the Cambridge University Society and on another evening, to see Rupert Brooke as Mephistopheles in the second production of the Marlowe Society's *Doctor Faustus*. This Daisy did not care for quite so much, but her capacity for enjoying herself and being pleased was astonishing. So was her ready sympathy, both for the characters and for the amateurs who played them. She had been to the theatre a good deal more often than Fred, but it was usually the halls, where if words deserted the half-drunk comic, the half-drunk audience were ready to supply them. Of *Doctor Faustus*, however, she did not know the words.

She asked Fred straight out about what Mr Wrayburn had said to her, though without mentioning *La Traviata*, and he told her that it was true. When they married he wouldn't be able to go on where he was. On the other hand, if she wouldn't have him, he didn't see that he would be able to go on at all.

Suddenly the whole Fairly family were in Cambridge. Hester telephoned the Cavendish. 'Look Hester, I'm not really supposed to – '

'I know, but the man at your college pretended not to know where you were.'

They were not at a hotel. That would be much too expensive. They were at the Anglican Hostel for Women of Limited Means, which also let in, said Hester, some Evangelicals.

'What have you done with Father?'

'He's staying in great comfort at Trinity Hall. He's to go to some dinner. That's really why we're here. It only happens every twenty-five years.'

'We told him we didn't grudge him anything,' Julia interrupted at full pitch. 'We said God grant you find some face, lad, you knew when all was young.'

'Is Mother there?'

'Freddie, my dear,' his mother said. 'I'm on my way to London. Rather an indirect route, you'll think, but we hope to get a glimpse of you. I have some prison visiting to do in London if we can get permission, and some clerical work, I daresay, for the Conciliation Bill. We are asking for votes for all women who pay more than ten pounds a year rent, provided the married ones don't vote in the same constituency as their husbands. That's just to keep Mr Asquith quiet. But please don't think that your mother is going to undertake anything spectacular.'

'Are the girls going with you?'

'No, Hester could be of some use, but Julia couldn't, and she is quite ready, you know, to admit it. Hester has offered to go back to Blow and look after both of them while I am away.'

'Mother, what have you been doing to my sisters? Their characters have changed.'

'Please don't distress yourself, Freddie.'

'Does Father know about all this?'

Julia came onto the line. 'We thought we would tell him tomorrow, when the dinner was over. He'll have indigestion by then and he'll have fallen out with all his friends, arguing about Christian Socialism. He'll be longing to come back to Blow with his two understanding daughters.'

'Julia, who is paying for this telephone call?'

'It's all written up on a notice. The hostel pays seven pounds a year for unlimited calls to subscribers within half a mile and one pound five shillings extra a year for every additional mile or fraction thereof. So, it's left to you, and you have to put whatever you think right in the mission box. They're profiteers, Freddie.'

'I'll be round as soon as I can.'

At the Anglican Hostel, where no-one might stay out later than nine o'clock, Fred told them that he had fallen in love. He spoke quietly, but caused uproar. Even Mrs Fairly raised her voice. The warden reminded them that from six to seven was supposed to be respected as a quiet hour and that guests were asked at all times to avoid controversial and unacceptable subjects.

'Who is she? Do we know her? Is she somebody's sister? Where did you meet her? When can we see her?'

'She doesn't have much time.' But Fred arranged, although it was so early in the year, to take them all out in a punt the following afternoon.

It was a day of thin sunshine. They met at the Chesterton boathouses and launched out on the shallow, placid Cam, the easiest punting, surely, in the world. Mrs Fairly sat with Hester, Julia with Daisy. Fred could see his mother's face and the back of Daisy's head. Recklessly he told himself that he loved them all. Let them find a way to love each other.

'We were delighted to have a chance of meeting you, Miss Saunders,' said Mrs Fairly, as they sat down. 'We have heard so very little about you.'

Hester frowned at her mother and said that Cambridge seemed very cold compared with their part of the country.

Fred punted slowly upstream. In telling them that Daisy was a nurse and came from London, he had told them pretty well all that he knew. Mrs Fairly tried again.

'Do you go much on the river in London, Miss Saunders?'

'Yes, I love the water,' said Daisy. 'You can have a good time on the Gravesend Ferry'. She added, 'Please do call me Daisy.'

Mrs Fairly said: 'I don't think my son mentioned your age?'

'I shall soon be twenty.'

'And you are a hospital nurse?'

'Really, Mother, do stop asking Daisy all these questions,' said Hester. 'You might be interviewing her for a vacancy.'

'I suppose she is in a way,' said Julia.

'Julia, that was quite ridiculous,' said Mrs Fairly sharply. 'I hope Miss Saunders is simply enjoying the fresh air, as I am.'

Fred had determined not to interfere. Pushing gently along up the bright spring river, he felt weightless, and almost careless. Now they were in the Backs, where from long habit, he began to call attention, to describe, and to point out – that willow overhanging the water, near the Wren Library, of course it will look better later in the year, (Mrs Fairly nodded, as she would have done in her own garden), that's John's, the Bridge of Sighs, then Clare, King's Bridge, King's of course, that red brick one is Queen's, rising straight out of the water, right out of its own reflection. How many times had his mother and sisters seen this stretch of the river and these buildings, on previous visits, before? But Daisy had never seen them and the rectory family, veterans of many parish outings, knew how to enjoy things unfamiliar to their guests as though for the first time.

Taking tea at the hostel after Fred had gone back to his lab and Daisy to her duties, Mrs Fairly returned to what Julia had said, 'or rather to the way you put it, Julia. A vacancy! Surely Fred can't even for a moment be thinking of leaving St Angelicus. And as to the girl herself – '

'Well, what about the girl herself?' Hester asked.

'You know I'm no respecter of persons, but can you imagine her in the parish?'

'I don't have to imagine her in the parish,' said Hester. 'I can imagine her selling *Votes for Women*.'

Julia told her mother that she was like the father in that opera.

'Which opera, Julia?'

Julia couldn't remember the name, which weakened the comparison, but she had thought Daisy looked splendid. Mr Fairly was not consulted on any of these points. Fred had asked him to dinner in hall that night and he had sat next to Professor Flowerdew who, with his melancholy smile, had told him that he could not hold out any great hopes for the future of the material universe. On the other hand, he had spoken very highly of Fred.

Part Four

Chapter Seventeen

DR MATTHEWS' GHOST STORY

Since the meeting of the Disobligers' Society Dr Matthews had been pondering over Fred's accident, and had come to regard it as much more mysterious than it really was. Wrayburn could tell him so little, but then Wrayburn (though he worked conscientiously) was a fool. He made a series of notes. – *The carter who was responsible for the accident has disappeared.* – One would assume that, having seen what he had done, he ran away. Not down the road, but into the open country. *What kind of country is it?* – Open, hedgeless country, with lines of willows marking the streams, such as you find in our inland fen country. *Where to hide?* – Very hard to say. We must assume that the carter either wanted to get to his home, or since that would hardly be the best place for someone being enquired for by the police, let us say to a safe friend. He was a local man, the farmer said, and our local men are not great travellers. He may have lodged in a barn, or between two potato clumps, but in the end he would have had to go back to the road, and proceed on foot. *But he was not seen on the road.*

What is to be done? If we want to find a man who has been seen on the road and has very positively been driving a cart, and has caused material damage to two bicycles, a man and a woman – but here I have to pause a while. *Was there not a third bicyclist?* And has he not too disappeared? And are we not told by our scientists and rationalists – who are perhaps not always the same people – that if we do not trust our senses, we have nothing left to trust? Those same five senses which are anointed by the Roman priest on a man's exit from this world and dismissed, so to speak, as having done their best for us (though we might ask, I think, do we always do our best for them? I met a man lately, a scientist, who had never smoked a pipe.)

I return to the carter. The carter could be heard, seen, shaken hands with and, I dare say, if he was an honest-day worker, he could also be smelled. Yet he was not found on the road, he was not found on either side of the road, or anywhere within many miles of it.

I believe, after all, that the best way to the truth may be to tell you a story. We shall have to proceed, you see, by analogy, which is a less respectable method than it used to be with theologians, but more respectable, I am told, with scientists. That is to say, I am going to compare the present moment with a past one, in the hope that it may throw a little light on our difficulties. I say this even although I do not much care for talking about, or even remembering, my experiences of forty-two years ago. You will have to see what you can make of them.

When I was a young man, I took part in any dig that was going, whether it was likely to lead to anything or not. You see, I was set in my bent very early, I mean the discoveries that can be made from old texts, and the discoveries that can be coaxed out of the earth itself and even more from brick and stone. One would say, a peaceful occupation enough. Anyway, it happened that our summer expedition of 1869 was, of all places, to the fields opposite what is now Mr Turner's farm – only there was no house near it then, and no Mr Turner – (the name at the farm was Hinton) – and, instead of the present road there was a cart-track across the fields which had been raised where it passed the farm gates into something like a bridge. It had been strengthened at that point with brickwork; after a summer storm, you could watch the sandmartins sliding in and out of the drainage holes, and I don't think I have ever seen so many swifts.

The bricks were very old, certainly mediæval. It had been

established by the man in charge of our little expedition, Edward Nisbet – (you will not remember him) – that between the second half of the thirteenth century and 1427 there had been a small nunnery at this unlikely spot. The nuns were Sisters of the Seven Sorrows. The dedication had been to St Salomé, the Virgin Mary's midwife. The farm, at the time, may well have been connected with the nunnery. All four of us stayed there, sleeping two and two in the four-posters in the garrets. The farmer's wife was pleased enough to have our custom. Selling eggs and poultry, and taking in passing guests, were the only extra money she could hope for, and how many people were likely to pass there in those days before the road was made?

'I hope you young gentlemen slept sound,' she asked us the first morning. We hastened to reassure her, except for Nisbet, who, while scrupulously polite, cared very much for accuracy.

'Nothing of great importance, but you and your friends were singing and talking very late, Mrs Hinton.'

– 'You mean me and Hinton? We're never late retiring. We work too hard for that.'

The rest of us, discerning a little resentment, or self-righteousness, here, said that we had heard nothing. I had slept in the same room as Nisbet, and I had certainly heard nothing.

We had paid Hinton to have the top-soil turned over before we came so that we could start our measurements and drawings at once. We had also hired two farmworkers, who gave it as their opinion that the site looked like nothing so much as a couple of rows of piggeries. The ground plan of the convent, to tell the truth, seemed likely to turn out to be nothing very particular. The only real interest of the place lay in an account given in 1426 of a special visitation ordered by the Bishop of Ely. At that time things were in an unsatisfactory state. There were only two very old women there who still wore the habit, though both were dirty and neglected, and a third who, though also old, was said to be of immoral life. The roof was described as 'not sufficient to keep out the rain'. The Bishop seems to have sent a second commissioner, empowered if necessary to evict the women and rehouse them in the convent of St Radegund. But the place was unimportant, and no further records survive. If the Bishop's visitor arrived, there is no means of knowing what happened to him. By the time the road was built there had been nothing for some three hundred years to show where once the nunnery stood. The grass covered it, the cattle moved over it.

Nisbet was no better the following night, when he actually woke me by dashing cold water in my face and told me that he could not only hear the voices but, quite distinctly, what was said.

'In, in, in', again and again, and once, 'in with him. Under, under, under.' The voices rose very high, higher than a woman's, he thought. They had been terrible to him.

The idea of some kind of joke on the part of Mrs Hinton arose, but to be rejected at once. Mrs Hinton laughed once and only once during one short stay, when one of our party tripped over the worn front doorstep of the farm kitchen and measured his length on the floor. Then she did laugh, in fact wept and wheezed with laughter. She didn't, she said, in the usual run, see anything like that from one year's end to the other, and it had done her good.

'One must be glad to have done our hostess good,' said Nisbet. 'I suppose, by the way, she can't be susceptible to rheumatism.'

'I suppose the whole Fen country is agueish,' I said.

'You don't feel a touch of it, Matthews?' – Did he? I asked.

'I'm in pain,' he answered, and now that I looked at him (it being a feature of living closely with anyone that you cease looking at them attentively) I saw that there was a leaden paleness, a darkness round his eyes and nostrils, which would normally be a symptom of the very ill.

'What sort of pain?'

'There is a pressure. I feel constricted.'

'That's in your mind, Nisbet.'

'It's not in my mind.'

'Let us get some fresh air.'

We went down to the diggings, although it was only just light. Nisbet at once suggested that we ought to open up the brickwork and the culverts in the ditch.

I have already referred to the culverts as being certainly as old as the convent. The field, of course, no longer relied on them for its drainage. Still, if they were dismantled, they would have to be put back, and neither of our farmworkers seemed very confident about being able to do this. To our astonishment, they both expressed the opinion that it was a bad thing to meddle about with old drainage work, and that there was no telling what was underneath it.

'But that's exactly what we're here for,' I said. 'That's what we're paying you for. We particularly want to know what is underneath it.'

They said they'd known jobs like that before, which had ended with the ground caving in and collapsing altogether. Pressed, they could not give the exact details. I am sure, however, that we should not have persisted with the idea if Nisbet had not shown such a sickly eagerness and a disposition, while the rest of us were at our surveying and note-taking, to linger round the culvert.

'Hang it,' the others said. 'He's nosing about like a dog round a sewer.'

He went out before we did, and came back later. Hoping to lighten the atmosphere, I asked him if he had seen anything in particular? To my surprise, he said he thought he had.

'Well, what, or whom?'

Reluctantly, he told me that it was an old woman, who had opened her mouth at him, as though gaping or gobbling. She was quite toothless. Now, forty years ago, old women without teeth were more common than not. If they were poor, they had no remedy. I asked him why he should care about that? He answered that he had been afraid she would touch him. I would have felt like laughing if he hadn't looked as he did.

'Where was she going?' I asked.

'To Guestingley, I suppose. There was nowhere else she could go.' He repeated, 'I was afraid she was going to touch me.'

I forget whether I mentioned that the other two members of our party were medical students. Although that by no means proved they knew anything very much, I decided to ask them something about the effects of strain, and whether we oughtn't to advise, or persuade, Nisbet to go home as soon as possible. Before I had the opportunity to do this, however, Nisbet told me that the night before, during which I must admit I had been sleeping soundly, he had got up and gone down to the ditch again to examine the brickwork in the bright moonlight.

'Well, and was your old woman there?'

He had seen three women, he said. They were down on hands and knees, poring at something large and dark which they had brought with them. It was the naked body of a man. The man was not dead, because there was some movement of the legs and feet. Then, by a process which Nisbet could not see, the man, whose bones must have been crushed and collapsed and his body distorted into a shape of grotesque length and thinness, was being inserted inch by inch into the culvert. He never made a sound, but the feet still moved.

– 'And what did they say, these women?'

– 'They said "in", "in", and then "under".'

'There'll be a moon tonight,' I said. 'I can't help feeling that it's a good deal easier to observe things by day, but if you want to do this night walking again, I shall come with you.'

He looked at me as if he couldn't remember exactly who I was. I should have said that by this time he was eating almost nothing, whereas the rest of us, after working all day in the open air, had very large appetites. We could not, of course, ask him not to sit at table with us, but it would have been much more pleasant if he had not. Mrs Hinton's feeling obviously was that he had paid for his board, so he ought to be given it. She put down great platefuls in front of him and took them away untouched without a word.

We went to our rooms and to bed.

'What the blazes are you doing?' I shouted, waking up suddenly. I had gone to sleep, and Nisbet, who had not undressed, was just going out of the room. I put on my Norfolk jacket and followed. Once outside the house, although normally Nisbet never ran, he began to run. I caught up with him at the same wretched place. He was lying down on the ditch, still damp and full of long weeds and grasses in the height of summer.

'I was waiting for you, Matthews.'

'Waiting for what? Have you found anything?'

'I wasn't looking for anything. I know what's there. My point is – have you got a sharp knife?'

'What for? I daresay I could fetch one from the kitchen.'

'All this should have been done in silence. You must cut my tongue out. That will be the work for you to do.'

I was determined to get him back to the farm. His mind seemed to have given way, which was a relief rather than otherwise. At that age I was reasonably strong. Rather stronger than Nisbet, perhaps. They talk about dragging people away, but how can you do it unless you can get hold of an arm or a leg? We were wrestling, both covered with grass and dirt. Nisbet repeated again and again, with an unpleasant tone of voice, 'In, in, sweetheart. In, in!'

– 'This won't do, old fellow,' I said. His 'in, in' made my flesh creep. I wasn't getting the better of him, and suddenly he reached over and stuck his right hand and half his arm in the culvert. It was a night of broken cloud and I could hardly see what I was doing. I got down and lay shoulder to shoulder with him, putting my left arm under his left armpit. Then I began to heave. It wasn't simply a question of his being caught or being stuck in the drain tunnel. Someone was hauling against me, stroke by stroke, to get him away.

'Pull together, Nisbet,' I shouted in his ear. 'Imagine we're both back at school. The tug-of-war, Nisbet, think of that. Heave!' I did not know where Nisbet had been at school, but I couldn't think of any other appeal to make. From what I could see, he was not looking much like a schoolboy. He was doing nothing to help me. He was doing his frantic best, in fact, to get free from me. Still 'in, in, in'. The only chance I had was when (as at last he did, lolling sideways) he fainted. Now the arm came out free, like a recoil. The hand had not gone, it was still joined at the wrist, but it was bones and tendons only. All the flesh had been dragged or sucked off to the last shreds. They had it all. I said aloud, 'He'll bleed to death.' But my shouting – 'Pull together', I suppose, and so forth, – must have been much louder than I knew and the other two fellows were running in their nightshirts down from the farm. I did not think of what they would feel when they saw poor Nisbet.

Neither of them had dealt before with a major haemorrhage, still, once he was on the kitchen table, they were able to manage a tourniquet. I fetched the doctor myself. I have forgotten now what explanation I gave. 'We are just on a quiet little expedition,' I said. 'During the summer vacation.' The doctor said he had never, in all his experience, been called in to an accident like this, particularly as the result of a quiet little expedition.

I do not know that you are ever likely to hear much more about this story. Certainly, Nisbet, although he recovered, was always very unwilling to talk about it. Because of his disability, he never took orders, for which he had been intended. Apart from the loss of his arm up to the elbow, there was some impairment to the brain. I believe he went to live abroad, I think in Belgium; yes, it was Belgium.

You will ask, what of the excavations? They were never taken in hand again, although there was necessarily some digging when the road was built. I made it my business at that time to find out whether anything worth noticing had been turned up. Yes, an ancient male skeleton, a curiosity, and rather a horrible one. It appeared to have been crushed and rolled up and then stretched or elongated. It was difficult to see how such a thing could have been carried out, particularly if it was done before the man was dead. There were a few rags of flesh, rather like the leather tongues of shoes; cured, you see, by the damp. To historians, much the most interesting items were some scraps of parchment which had been thrust or stuffed at some point, in a quite unseemly way, into the corpse. The few letters (there were no complete words) which could be deciphered made it almost certain that these scraps were part of a *quoniam igitur* – a writ of eviction issued by the Bishop, following on a second visit and inspection. You must remember that although there are more than ten thousand mediæval writs of *significavit* in the Public Record Office, there was, up to that time, not a single example of a *quoniam igitur*. You will understand, therefore, the historians' excitement. But it must be said that historians, in my experience, are excitable people.

And now you will want me to return to my analogy. However, it is not quite that, after all. We set out to discuss the whereabouts of an unfortunate carter and of the third bicyclist, who had also disappeared. They were not found on the road, or by the road, the police assure us of that. But tell me, should we not also look *under* the road? I do not mean that the carter and the bicyclist have been the victims of any human violence. Buried, however, beneath the tarmac, where the ancient brick culvert runs, I believe, they are. Peace to what remains of them! We talk of 'vanishing into thin air'. They, however, have been swallowed by gross earth and fen water. There are places, not always impressive, or even noticeable in themselves, which cannot be disturbed. Something so loathsome or so cruel has once happened there, that any disturbance will demand a repetition – we may call it a reparation in human blood. When, and how often? Well, it is not for us to know the times and the places. Let each of us lay a hand on his heart and consider whether he has been, at some time or another, in a place which appears not to have settled down peacefully, but seems, on the contrary, to be waiting to be laid to rest. The carter and the bicyclist are gone. Let us say that it's happened. I have been asked, not once, but often, do I believe these things? Well, I can only say that I am prepared to consider the evidence, and accept it if I am satisfied.

Dr Matthews' story was written. Where and to whom should it be read aloud? This was the second part of his usual exorcism of whatever lay on his mind. It was his habit to wait until October, for the Feast of All Souls and All Saints, when the past year's dead are invited to return from their uncanny kingdom to their old places, and to sit at their own table. He often read aloud at this season to the Burrowers, a society for mediæval palaeographers. But he did not feel like waiting for their next meeting.

'A singular impatience,' he said to himself. Crossing the Protector's Court at St James's with his manuscript in his pocket, he met the Junior Dean.

'Ah, Hartley!' Hartley could scarcely refuse to spare his Provost half an hour. The two of them went back to Dr Matthews' house. When the reading was over – Dr Matthews read deliberately, imitating each voice in turn – he paused, and looked searchingly through his round glasses.

'I enjoyed that very much, Provost,' said the Junior Dean. There was silence, which couldn't be what was required, so he added, 'There was a certain symbolism in it, I thought, and perhaps a hint of sex.'

'I hope there is nothing of the kind. I never make alterations in my stories, once written, and I shan't alter this one. Still, as I say, there is, I hope, nothing of the kind. Sex is tiresome enough in novels. In a ghost story, I should have no patience with it.'

'Surely if one doesn't find sex tiresome in life, it won't be tiresome in fiction,' said the Junior Dean.

'I *do* find it tiresome in life,' Dr Matthews replied. 'Or rather, I find other people's concern with it tiresome. One is told about it and told and told!'

The Junior Dean did not think he had repeated the story to anyone. It circulated, however, and with it the rumour that the Provost of St James's believed there was someone – perhaps two people – buried quite recently underneath the Guestingley Road, just a few miles before you come to Dr Sage's lunatic asylum. After a while, the tale elaborated itself with the addition that the police were considering an application to close the road while they made a preliminary search – that, of course, would mean a considerable detour for horse and motor traffic. The police, who had taken no action on the Guestingley Road incident, because they couldn't see how to proceed, were well aware that the Provost, though cranky, carried weight, and was known often to go up to London, where he was consulted by influential people. Perhaps he was not very likely on these occasions to talk about the disappearing carter, but they decided in any case to put an end to a troublesome business. A summons was served on George Turner, farmer, for having provided a carter or driver, with whom he had a master and servant relationship, with an unsafe vehicle not showing front lights or rear lights, as specified by the Roadway Lighting Act of 1904 and also holding him responsible as an employer for the wrongs committed by his employee who, on March 2nd 1911, drove the above-mentioned cart without reasonable care and foresight, causing injuries to Frederick Aylmer Fairly and Daisy Saunders and damage to their machines. The magistrate's clerk wrote to Turner to ask him whether he proposed to appear in court, or whether he would be represented by a solicitor. Turner sent a message to say: both. The police gave up hope that the whole thing would be not much more than a formality. They summoned Fred, Daisy and Mrs Wrayburn as witnesses.

'They won't need you dear,' said Mrs Wrayburn to her husband. 'There is nothing for you to worry about.'

'I imagine they know my time is valuable. They may be aware that I'm overwhelmed with work. I'm surprised that they've got so much sense. If they had tried to make me attend, I should have been obliged to refuse. And if, as a result, they had seen fit to arrest me, I should have been ready, on a point of principle, to face prison. The suffragettes need not think they have the monopoly of that.'

He was not called upon, and continued to complain.

Chapter Eighteen

AN UNUSUAL COURT CASE

The court opened at ten, before the lately appointed stipendiary magistrate. Fred, Daisy and Mrs Wrayburn were told to wait in the witnesses' room. The proceedings were not expected to take long, and Daisy had her things in a bag ready to bicycle to the hospital. She seemed very pale. Her face was still fresh, but she looked blindly, as a statue does, not being given any feelings to show. Gallant Mrs Wrayburn, in crimson Russian boots and a linen tabard, did her best to encourage both of them by suggesting (the room was small and stuffy) that they had all been mistaken for prisoners and would be soon given their skilly and required to sew mailbags.

'Mrs Wrayburn, I can't smile,' said Daisy, 'and the Lord knows how you can. If you hadn't done a good action and picked us up off the road, you wouldn't have to be wasting your time here this morning. Don't you think about that?'

'Perhaps a little,' said Mrs Wrayburn.

The witnesses were not allowed into court until George Turner had been charged. An inspector from the station appeared to conduct the prosecution. 'Your name is Richard Catcher, you are a detective sergeant,' he had read out rapidly to his first witness. 'Did you, on the 4th of April, interview Mr George Turner at Turner's farm, Guestingley Road, and did you charge him with the two offences, and did he become abusive and show signs of endeavouring to hinder you in the execution of your duty, and did he ask you why you had not found the missing carter, and state that the Cambridgeshire police had less idea how to find anyone than a bitch chasing fleas on her own arse?' The sergeant had agreed to this.

Fred was sworn in and taken through his evidence. It was the first time he had seen George Turner, who sat there intransigent, his neck shrunken by the east winds inside his hard Sunday collar, his hands on his knees, a blameless, simple man bewildered by the processes of the law. The defence solicitor, who got up to cross-examine, appeared anxious to earn his money. He asked Fred whether he had good eyesight. Fred said that he had. The solicitor looked disconsolate. Had it been pitch dark? No, but dark enough.

'Mr Fairly,' said the solicitor, 'do you consider yourself a scientist and a philosopher?'

The magistrate asked whether this was material to the case. The solicitor said he was questioning the witness's reliability.

'I've never been a philosopher,' said Fred. 'If you mean, as I think you do, that as a scientist, I'm not able to look where I'm going, then I must tell you that you're mistaken.'

Mrs Wrayburn, after Fred had sat down, was sworn in, and told that she was a housewife. 'I should be a graduate,' she said, 'if the university allowed women to take degrees.'

'Mrs Wrayburn, you are a housewife,' the inspector went on. 'On the night of February the 26th you heard what sounded like a collision outside your house. You put on a waterproof and, going out into the road, discovered two individuals, a man and a woman lying apparently injured. You were not at that time able to identify them. You then went for assistance to the neighbouring farm and found Mr Turner's son, who conveyed the two victims to your house one at a time on a handcart.'

'Is Mr Turner's son in court?' asked the magistrate. The son had been excused because he had been taken poorly. He had been allowed to put in a sworn statement, in the course of which he stated that he didn't know who his father had hired to drive the cart or whether it had lights or not. But he reckoned it must have had some or how would the driver have been able to see?

'You were lucky to have got as much sense as that out of him,' called out George Turner.

The magistrate told him that he would have the opportunity to speak later. 'I've got plenty to say,' replied Turner.

Every time Fred saw Daisy he was taken off guard and, although it seemed to him he never forgot anything about her, he was overwhelmed by all that, after all, he had not remembered quite correctly. The evidence, so far, had only taken twenty minutes or so. Twenty minutes or so ago, then, he had been sitting with her in the witnesses' waiting-room. He had noticed then that she was pale, but now he saw that he hadn't given proper attention to the kind of pallor, something more like a white tea-rose, where the colour is below the surface and can only just be guessed at. While Fred (totally oblivious of Mach's principle that the element of wonder never lies in the phenomenon, but always in the person observing) raved on to himself like this, Daisy was sworn in.

'Mr Fairly has said earlier on in evidence that you were riding either side by side with, or just behind, another bicyclist,' the inspector began, 'a man, who would naturally have been a witness to the accident. You must, of course, have seen this man, and there is a possibility that you know him. Now, Miss Saunders, could you tell the court his name, or give us any other information about him?'

'No, I couldn't,' said Daisy.

'You don't know who he was?'

'No, I don't.'

'You are a friend or an acquaintance of this man?'

'No.'

'But you were bicycling with him?'

'I was cycling behind him.'

The magistrate said he would like to clarify the point. He, too, had noticed Daisy's pallor, but attributed it to menstrual trouble. Since he very much disliked having anyone fainting in court, he tried to rally her a little.

'The police, you know, Miss Saunders, have not been successful in tracing this man. Have you any idea where he might be found?'

'If I don't know who he is, how can I know where he's gone?' Daisy cried.

'That doesn't follow, Miss Saunders.'

'The defendant is entitled to testify on his own behalf,' said the magistrate.

'I've plenty to say,' George Turner repeated, 'but my lawyer here tells me there's no case to answer.'

'Is that your submission?'

'Yes, that's my submission, according to the laws of the land.'

'I don't need instruction about the laws of the land,' said the magistrate. 'Is that all you have to say?'

'What I am telling you is that you can't hold me responsible for someone you can't lay hands on, and none of us can't remember what his surname is. Why, there's a professor walking about Cambridge at the moment saying that this man, the one who was driving the cart, I mean, that he's lying dead and buried under the Guestingley Road.'

As George Turner made this last remark in a tone which suggested he was telling a joke, his solicitor allowed himself a smile. Turner sat down, folding his arms. The inspector got to his feet and reminded the magistrate that the police now had some additional evidence. The magistrate and his clerk bent towards each other and murmured in harmony.

'You want to put in a written statement?'

'I can call the witness in person, your worship. He got here ten minutes ago.'

A constable was sent to the waiting room and Kelly walked into the court. He was wearing a fawn waistcoat, like a tipster's, and looked ill and savage. As he gazed about him, knowing and experienced, there was for the first time in the court a physical sensation, like hot breath close to the cheek, of guilt and danger.

Kelly gave his occupation as a newspaper editor and journalist. The magistrate, who was becoming short-tempered, said that surely one implied the other. Kelly did not reply. He stared straight in front of him, licking his lips as though thirsty. Asked where he was on the evening of February the 26th, he replied that he was coming out of Cambridge, cycling in the direction of Guestingley. – Did he in fact reach Guestingley? No, he didn't. He'd only just about missed being hit by a horse and cart and he had had to swerve clean across to the right of the road.

The magistrate said: 'I want to know if you can describe or identify the driver of the cart.'

'Yes, I can. When he saw what he had done he jumped off the driver's seat and ran off towards the farmhouse. I saw him in the light of my headlamp.'

'Can you describe him?'

'I don't need to do that. He's here.' He jerked his head towards Turner. 'He was driving the cart.'

Turner bellowed and was escorted bellowing out of the court, but could be heard from the corridor outside with the constable calmly arguing restraint, and then less calmly.

'I shall dismiss this case until the summons is amended,' said the magistrate. 'Please tell them to make a great deal less noise outside the court, and if necessary to take the defendant into detention. Meanwhile I shall take one or two additional points. Mr Kelly, what exactly did you do after the accident?'

'I turned back to Cambridge and went to Pett's Hotel. I had a room booked there for the night for Daisy Saunders and myself. I knew she would have to come back there eventually. She hadn't any money and her cycle was smashed.'

'Are you referring to Miss Saunders, who is at present in court as a witness?'

'Yes, Daisy Saunders. I got gypped, though. She didn't turn up until the following morning.'

'Why did you not report the accident immediately, in case help was needed?'

'I wanted to keep out of it. I didn't want it to get about we were going to a hotel together. I didn't want to cock it all up for her.'

Kelly was speaking so quietly and flatly that the magistrate and his clerk were both leaning forward, their usual reproach to the indistinct. The magistrate repeated:

'You did not wish to cock it all up for Miss Saunders. I take it that you mean you did not wish to embarrass her. What has made you decide to come forward now? Please speak plainly.'

'I've changed my mind,' said Kelly. Then he shouted: 'Jesus' eyes, now I do want to cock it all up for her.'

Chapter Nineteen

KELLY LAID TO REST

Mr Turner's solicitor retrieved him, and he was bound over, pending further enquiries. Kelly was detained by the police, who required him to make a signed deposition. All the others were free to go. Daisy took her bag and departed for Dr Sage's hospital. She had not looked even once at Kelly, although his eyes had been fixed on her. Neither had she spoken to Fred.

Fred went and sat for three hours in a small café in front of the magistrate's court. He ordered a cup of tea and two biscuits for five pence and thought of nothing. – Oh, but that's impossible. – It's not possible to think of nothing. Certainly it was unprofessional of Fred, who was paid by the university to use his mind, and unwise of him as a lover, but there it was, he was occupied with bitter sensations, giving way to stupefaction, then to emptiness.

The café was really only the front room of a small house. A coal fire smoked in a dispirited grate – not coal exactly, but brickettes made of coal dust and tea-leaves. There were three tables only. The manageress came through a bead curtain and asked if she should light the gas. Unless Fred wanted to read, she would keep it low. Fred recognised the note, universal as the voice of the sea, of worry about money.

'I don't want to read,' he said. 'Really, I don't need the gas at all.'

'Oh, I don't want to look as though I wasn't open. In fact, I was going to ask if you'd sit by the window, to give some atmosphere, you see, if anyone's passing.'

Fred went and sat by the window. She moved his cup and

plate after him. 'Your tea's cold now, I'm afraid. I would have drawn your attention to it before, only I was afraid you were thinking.'

'Do you get a lot of thinkers in here?' he asked.

'We don't get a lot of anyone. You'd think it would be a good place, opposite the court and the police station. Perhaps, though, if they see you talking – it would be better, really, if you could smile a bit. I could tell my father to come in here and sit with you at your table, only he doesn't have very good hearing.'

Fred tried to smile.

'Didn't you fancy your biscuits?' she asked.

'Look,' said Fred, 'if the police keep someone in there to ask him questions and so on, then when they let him out, surely he'd cross the road and come in here?'

'No, he wouldn't,' said the manageress's father, rattling and tottering in through the bead curtain, not seeming at all deaf. 'He wouldn't come over here. If they're detained by the police they all get away as quick as possible.'

'I'm waiting for someone to come out. That's what I'm sitting here for,' said Fred.

'Will you be ordering something further, then?' asked the manageress.

'Yes, yes, the same again.'

'You wouldn't prefer something on toast?'

'Yes, the same again, but on toast.'

'You'll want some for your friend?'

'I don't want anything for him. He's not my friend. I'm not really the sort of person you hoped for, I'm afraid.'

'I'd looked for young people,' she said doubtfully.

'I'm twenty-five, nearly twenty-six,' he said. She looked more doubtful still.

'But your friend might want something on toast?'

'I don't want to order anything for him. I don't even want to speak to him.'

'You've waited three hours for him. I should have thought it was worth while speaking to him.'

'I want to hit him.'

Fred realised now what it was that he had not been thinking about. The old father laughed extravagantly, steadying himself by holding onto the back of a chair. Fortunately Fred had a reasonable amount of money on him, having hoped to take out Daisy and, if necessary, Mrs Wrayburn, to luncheon. While paying for his various orders he saw Kelly coming down the steps of the police-station and felt a peculiar shock of disbelief that comes when the long awaited arrives. Kelly had his hat pulled forward instead of on the back of his head and his jacket collar turned up. It must be raining a little. When he reached the pavement he turned right and began to walk with his usual strut, which seemed to Fred to be that of a man who felt he had unlimited access to women, so that a young girl, picked up by chance and taken for the night to a cheap hotel, would be as nothing. His jacket would matter more to him, being less easy to replace.

There was nothing to discuss. Fred sprinted across the road behind a motorcycle and in front of a dray, caught up with Kelly, grasped him by the coat collar, and spun him round. This left them both in an unmanageable position, with Fred's arm round the back of his neck, locked in an embrace.

'You're the schoolteacher,' said Kelly. He turned his head as far as he could and spat in Fred's face. 'Shock off, schoolteacher.' Fred changed grip and hit him hard just below the ear. It was not a fair blow, but justice is sometimes what you can afford. Kelly did not behave at all as Fred expected. He stood for a moment as though doubtful whether to fall to the left or the right and then collapsed deliberately and totally as though only his jacket had been holding him together. He fell in front of a shop, a repairing tailor's, and lay there unmoving.

'Do you need a hand, Fairly?' It was Skippey, quite unexpected at this end of Cambridge. 'There's a man, you know, lying on the pavement quite close to you.' Passers-by, not wishing to be involved, made a detour to avoid them.

'Yes, I knocked him over.'

'Do you regret it?'

'No, I don't regret it.'

'But I think he can't stay here, Fairly.' Skippey picked up Kelly's feet, in their worn sharply pointed boots. 'Where to?'

'Honestly, Skippey, I don't know.'

'Something will suggest itself as we go.'

Skippey walked in front with his back towards Kelly, holding him under the knees. In this way they successfully crossed Parker's Piece. He talked quietly but incessantly over his shoulder to Fred, who followed, supporting Kelly's head and shoulders, and looking after his hat.

'Fairly, this whole incident is not characteristic of you.'

'I'll tell you who he is. I'll tell you what he tried to do.'

'Later, later. I'm glad to have come across you, as a matter of fact, because I should like to discuss a problem I've run into.'

They continued to thread their way down St Andrew's Street between people on other business.

'I'm working,' Skippey continued, 'as you know, on the Michelson-Morley experiments. I think the whole series could be repeated still more accurately. Minute changes of length, of course, entailing very fine measurements, which I can hardly be expected to undertake entirely by myself if I'm to perform my other duties satisfactorily. Yet I'm getting no response at all from my repeated requests for an assistant.'

They negotiated a corner, where Kelly's hat fell, and was retrieved by a schoolboy. The rain was still falling gently.

'It's not that there are no funds available, there is always money to spare in a great university. Extensions, medical schools, they're building in all directions. They all want libraries put up, even the parasitologists, yes, Fairly, even the economists. Yes! And gold seems to rain on them from the skies. Yet I'm not satisfied that my application has ever been read, much less considered.'

'Perhaps they don't feel much more needs doing on Michelson-Morley.'

'Ah, Fairly! But I'm not satisfied that they offered anything like a complete proof.'

'I don't see that a complete proof is possible,' said Fred. He couldn't believe that Kelly could remain unconscious for this length of time, unless he was very seriously hurt, and he didn't believe that either. His colour was better now than it had been in court. Perhaps, like a baby, he simply liked being carried about.

'I'm not just talking about the interferometer, you know, Fairly. I'm talking about the Fitzgerald-Lorenz contradictions.'

Skippey's high-pitched flow of words reassured everyone they passed. Either these were two good companions, carrying a friend who had drunk too much, or they were conducting an experiment in weights and measures which must have escaped from the bounds of the laboratories. The two of them might, it seemed, go on walking and talking indefinitely with their unusual load. To Fred's surprise, however, Skippey had a perfectly good notion of where he was going. As they passed the Botanic Gardens he made a sharp swing to the right and in through the public entrance.

'I want to see Batty. Perhaps you've met him – botanic morphology and homology.'

'Why?'

'I may catch him in one of the greenhouses. I want to get him to speak next week at the Disobligers' Society. I'd like him to speak for the motion that we'd be far better off without trees.'

Meanwhile it was nearly closing time. The gardens were almost empty. The grass had been mown for the first time that spring and near the verge of the wide lawns a large wire basket stood, full of green clippings.

'In here, I think,' said Skippey, preoccupied. Then, as Kelly was lowered into the yielding lap of the grass, he added: 'A reasonable standard of comfort, I think.'

Chapter Twenty

FRED'S ADVICE TO HIS STUDENTS

One of Fred's problems was that he had to give a talk in about ten minutes' time to his first-year second-term practical physics students. Pursued to the last moment by Skippey, who wished to continue their discussion, he took a taxi to St Angelicus to fetch his gown. From the Porter's Lodge he telephoned the Botanic Gardens. He did not want to speak to the curator, he explained, it was a matter for the head gardener. Had there been, or was there a man asleep, or perhaps taken ill in the large grass basket on the south-east side of the lawns? The head gardener went away for what seemed a very long time to make his enquiries. Yes, there had been a man. They'd found him in the basket at closing time. Where was he now? They couldn't say. He'd run for it. Had he looked ill? Not too ill to climb the fence, it seemed.

In Fred's room there was as usual a small pile of cards, invitations and letters. One was from Holcombe. 'After the court rose this morning, I was, as so often, not able to find you. That is why I'm writing this. You did not notice me, I think, at the back of the public gallery, but I was there. What I had intended to say to you was a continuation, in a sense, of my last note to you, also written on the night of a Disobligers' Meeting. In that I congratulated you, avoiding, I hope, any bitterness, on your freedom, as a Junior Fellow of St Angelicus, from any serious emotional worry. There was no point at all, I reminded you, on your getting to know any young women at all of the marriageable class. Well, I've seen your Miss

Saunders now, and it is only too evident that, although good-looking, she is not of the marriageable class. You, I imagine, cannot, after what passed, possibly intend to see her again, but, Fairly, you've no idea how difficult it is for me to get hold of a woman of any kind. Here is my suggestion. I cannot afford to marry, but neither can I afford to be particular and nor, I suppose, can Miss Saunders. . . .'

Fred took his gown from its hook on the back of the door and walked to the Cavendish.

There were eight undergraduates sitting where he himself had sat eight years ago, glad to be young, and pitying the light-heartedness of the middle-aged. Then, as now, J. J. Thomson was in charge at the Cavendish (although he had become Sir Joseph), then, as now, the labs were overcrowded with research students, all of them left to patch up their own apparatus by trial and error, each of them lucky if they could find a little space, even on a single table. The room at the very top of the building where Fred lectured was (now as then) icy cold because of the very narrow bore of the copper heating pipes which were supposed to avoid magnetic disturbance. Out of this squalor had come indisputable greatness. Not one of the students would have wished to be anywhere else on earth. They were at the Cavendish.

Fred was a good teacher, having begun early by helping out at Sunday School. All the village children of Blow attended every Sunday afternoon. It was their parents' only chance, in the crowded cottages, to get to bed with each other without interruption. This was well understood at the Rectory. Fred, and Mrs Fairly, and later on, Hester, knew that rain or shine, they must keep hard at it in the parish room till half past three. 'What was the second plague of Egypt?' 'What was made of Shittim wood overlaid with gold?' 'When Balaam's ass was endowed with speech, what was her first remark?' It was strange to think how many village children in England, certainly in Blow, could answer these questions without hesitation.

Fred told his class that he would conclude this afternoon with Gauss's theorem as applied to gravitational fields. 'The total outward normal gravitational flux over any surface enclosing a mass m is equal to $4 \pi m$. The 4π occurs here because we are using a non-rationalised system, and the negative sign because the gravitational field always acts towards a point mass.'

For some reason the class found it necessary to take all this down. There was an element of sympathetic magic here. When the last one had stopped writing and the lid of the last inkwell had been shut, Fred said, 'Just a moment. Two weeks ago I asked you to write an essay. I have your papers here, but I'm not going to give them back for the moment because I am not quite satisfied with them. "Not quite satisfied" is, of course, what we say in this university for "not at all satisfied". You remember I asked you to write a general essay. If I was proposing a subject to you to-day it would very probably not be the same one, but as it was I asked you to devise a rational system of measuring human happiness. All of you looked startled. A physicist sitting down to answer such a question, you seemed to think, would be a freak. As a class, you had the air of wanting your money back. I, however, wanted to have the opportunity of reminding you that there is no difference whatever between scientific thought and ordinary thought. We know something about the physiology of the memory and something about the physiology of the senses, but we don't yet understand the physiology of thought. Believe me, when we do understand it we shall find that all thinking is done in precisely the same way.

'Whatever you do, gentlemen, don't, as scientists, believe you are anything extraordinary. Don't allow yourself for a moment to feel anything like contempt for those whose minds work differently from your own. Their minds in fact don't work differently from your own. Don't tell yourself that their ideas are commonplace. It's very good for an idea to be commonplace. The important thing is that a new idea should develop out of what is already there so that it soon becomes an old acquaintance. Old acquaintances aren't by any means always welcome, but at least one can't be mistaken as to who or what they are.

'You have come to Cambridge to study the interdependence of matter and energy. Please remember that energy and matter are in no way something distinct from yourselves. Remember, too, that scientists are not dispassionate. Your judgement and your ability to do good work will be in part dependent on your digestion, your prejudices and above all, your emotional life. You must face the fact that if another human being, whose welfare means considerably more to you than your own, behaves in a very different way from anything you had expected, then your efficiency may be impaired. When the heart is breaking, it is nothing but an absurd illusion to think you can taste the blood. Still I repeat, your efficiency may be impaired.'

The undergraduates in their black or dark blue gowns, went murmuring out of the cold, cramped room. Two of them turned and stayed behind, intercepting Fred.

'You said, Mr Fairly, that our essays were very bad.' He was Robert Cork, Sidney Sussex, and that was Fraill, from Pembroke.

'Well, they were very bad. But I'm going to find an opportunity to discuss them later on with each one of you personally.'

Cork took a deep breath. 'Perhaps you wouldn't mind my saying that I was worried by your last remarks this afternoon. Fraill, here, too, was worried. Your remarks distressed us. They seemed to go beyond the impersonal. We both feel we benefit from your teaching and to some extent we have taken you as a model for the early stages of the scientist's life.'

'What do you want a model for?' asked Fred, but Cork only repeated: 'We were worried,' while Fraill boldly put in: 'It sounded something like a personal trouble.'

'Your papers were very bad, both of them,' said Fred. 'However, thank you.'

Chapter Twenty-One

AT DR SAGE'S HOSPITAL

Dr Sage's hospital (his partner's name, whatever it was, was never mentioned) had once been a large private house. It was a rose-pink Jacobean-style mansion with Dutch gables and odd-looking oriel windows which the virginia creeper and wisteria partly hid. Fred asked his cab to wait. He still had another appointment that evening which couldn't be cancelled or deferred. That meant arriving back in Cambridge by seven.

At the reception desk he said: 'I should like to speak to Miss Saunders. She is one of the nurses here.'

'There's none of them called that, sir.'

At the same time Dr Sage himself, coming, with a welcome touch of wildness, out of his private office, shouted: 'Here I am, if you want me! There's nothing wrong, you know, with my patients here! Wrong in fact doesn't describe any of them. I can easily imagine a society in which they would be quite normal. Not so easy to imagine one in which they would be happy.'

'This gentleman is enquiring for a Nurse Saunders, Doctor. But we haven't a nurse of that name.'

'Saunders is here, but she's not a nurse,' said Dr Sage sharply. 'She is a ward-maid. You ought to have known that. Don't, in your ignorance, amuse yourself by turning away my callers. You are the receptionist. Receive!' He disappeared out of the front door. A porter was sent for to take Fred to the service entrance.

'You can't go in there until they come out,' he explained.

'When do they get off work?'

'Half-six, sir.'

The service entrance was the old back door of the house. Out of the high window above it came gusts of disinfectant, gravy, custard and Monkey Brand soap. Round the corner of the building Fred could see a green lawn where Dr Sage, calm now, was pacing gravely to and fro, to and fro, with a gesticulating patient.

Women began to come out in twos and threes, carrying the bags they had brought with them for their allowance of hospital scraps. The lights went on. How much of the day have I spent waiting? Fred asked himself. Then at last Daisy appeared, wearing her coat, but not her hat. He was taken off guard.

'Well, you've caught me out,' she said flatly. 'Dr Sage didn't give me a nurse's place. Of course he didn't. I never even got my certificate. He's still at the Blackfriars three days a week. He knows what happened to me. I didn't have any explaining to do. That was a relief. He said he'd take me on for the ironing. We have a lot of incontinents here. We use more linen than most.'

'That's not what I want to ask you about, Daisy.'

'I didn't think you'd come out here,' she said.

'I shall always come where you are. How could you not know that? But, Daisy –'

'Well, what?'

'It's all horrible. Pett's Hotel is horrible. You can take rooms there by the hour.'

'Well, that's handy for some,' said Daisy.

'Don't talk like that,' he said.

'Well, I never went there. I was going to, but as it turned out, I didn't.'

'But Daisy – he's horrible as well. Kelly is horrible.'

'Perhaps he wouldn't do for Cambridge, but it takes all sorts.'

'Not that sort, in heaven's name, how could you go to Cambridge or anywhere else with one of that sort?'

'If you want to know, I'll tell you. I felt down. I told you how I lost my place. I didn't count on meeting Kelly at Liverpool Street. I didn't count on meeting anyone. But when he was there, even though he was dressed flash and I didn't like him, still he was better than no-one.'

'But do you love him, Daisy?'

'Lord, no.'

Fred had a suffocating feeling that there were laws or regulations governing his situation so that only a certain number of questions would be allowed. Also, that he was already asking the wrong ones.

'Why did you say in court that you didn't know who he was?'

He wanted to get her away from the back door. They were standing under a gas standard which dimly lit up the path. She looked very pale and not, perhaps, even pretty. Why had she said she didn't know who Kelly was? That, indeed, was what Fred most needed to be told. It was just within the bounds of the possible that she had pretended not to know this man with the idea of sparing his own feelings. If that was so, the whole towering structure of his misery would disintegrate, leaving only what was precious behind. Say it, Daisy, say it, say it. But he dared not ask her.

'Of course I don't tell lies unless I've got to,' she said. 'Any more than you run to catch a tram unless you've got to.'

Say it, say it.

'I was afraid he might turn up here,' she said, almost as though making conversation. 'I don't see as he'd want to go back to London. Unless the police kept him, I don't know where he can have got to.'

'My God, you don't care where he's got to, do you?'

She murmured something which he couldn't hear, except for the word 'better'. He said bitterly: 'Don't put yourself to any trouble. If you are worried about him, I can set your mind at rest. He is, or was, until a short time ago, in a rubbish bin at the Botanic Gardens.'

Daisy looked frightened.

'I had to knock him down, Daisy.'

'You mean you knocked him out?'

'Not exactly.'

'Kelly's older than you, quite a bit. His hair's dyed. You must have noticed that if you got close to him. He has to pretend to be young in his line of business. His job's nothing to be proud of, but then he didn't have your advantages. You think of that the next time you come across a poor sod like Kelly.'

They looked at each other in despair, and now there seemed to be another law or regulation by which they were obliged to say to each other what they did not mean and to attack what they wished to defend. Out of the dusk the hospital porter cleared his throat.

'I'm sorry, sir, it isn't the doctor who wants to lock up, he wants to keep the whole place open, night and day, but the Board says we've got to.'

Daisy said: 'Don't come here again, Fred. I'm not going to be here. You won't find me here.'

'But is that true, Daisy? Is it the truth?'

He knew that it was. Daisy went back through the kitchen entrance and shut the door behind her.

Chapter Twenty-Two

THE GATE OF ANGELS

That was at seven. At half-past Fred, as had been arranged, called in on Professor Flowerdew. He apologised for not being quite himself.

'Not at all, my dear Fairly. I know what has been happening to you. You've been giving evidence, haven't you, in, of all things, the police court. The Provost of James's asked me in, an hour or so ago, for a glass of sherry. Although he dines here fairly often, I think I'm the only member of the Faculty of Natural Sciences with whom he is on sherry-drinking terms. And that is only because he believes, quite wrongly, that I am opposed to experimental research. He told me, in any case, about your distressing experiences this morning.'

'Do you mean that Dr Matthews was in court?'

'He went to watch the proceedings, it seems – why, I can't think.'

'I didn't see him,' said Fred.

Dr Matthews, Holcombe, how many more? He hadn't noticed them and if he had, they would have meant nothing to him. His mind would not have had room for them.

'A most distinguished scholar,' the Professor went mildly on, 'but they say that he hears rapping and tapping behind the panelling of the Provost's house. Well, a man, of course, has a right to hear rapping and tapping in his own college. Anyway, he spoke to me of unpleasant characters making an appearance in court – a seedy young man, a rather difficult farmer, a pretty, but dishonest young woman.'

'I don't think you should take everything Dr Matthews says on trust,' said Fred with an effort. 'He's a writer of fiction, as of course you know.'

'Yes,' said Professor Flowerdew doubtfully. 'He must find it very confusing.'

Fred had come, as part of his absolute duties, to collect his professor and take him to an Evening Discourse given (to mark its importance) in the east room of the Old Schools. The subject, in its way, was a delicate one. It was to be an explanation of how Ernest Rutherford, still in Manchester, had come to find himself in disagreement with his old master, J. J. Thomson, as to the structure of the atom and as to what – if anyone could see it – it would look like. Rutherford himself had not been able to come, but he had sent down from Manchester his personal assistant, Hans Geiger, and, as demonstrator, a very young research student called Marsden.

'I shan't go to hear them,' said Professor Flowerdew, 'but I shall be grateful if you could take very complete notes, which I do not think will be distributed in a typed or printed form at the lecture. Rutherford has proposed a nuclear atom. In that, there is nothing at all remarkable. Newton proposed it himself, although it was one of the occasions when he neglected his own principles. Rutherford, however, claims to be able to show that it exists, that this unobservable, consisting of unobservables, depending on exchanges of energy of which he can only say that he has no idea when or why they may take place, exists, and that we must take it to be the indivisible unit of matter.'

Fred wanted only to be alone, but he said, 'You ought to come, Professor.'

'No, Fairly, I might disgrace myself. I might ask, "How can the unobservable be indivisible?" or, indeed, divisible, for that too, I daresay, will soon be proposed.'

'Well, I'll go and see what they say. I don't know how long it will go on.'

'No matter how long, call in again immediately when you get back to college.'

'Do you want me to wait for the questions?'

Flowerdew wavered a little. 'Not for too many.'

There was a hint of coming weakness in his voice, just as the Cambridge autumn can be felt even before one leaf falls, when the wind from the fens turns from cold to colder. Professor Flowerdew would never change his mind, that was not possible for him. It was not that he supported J. J. Thomson's orderly atom against Rutherford's wild, airy and fractious one. To him, both these great intellects were pursuing nothings. Like Benedict XIII himself, he might be asked to admit defeat, but would never recognise it as legitimate, or even respectable. He might find it necessary to retreat even farther into seclusion. He might, even, have to apply for a post at Oxford, but if this should happen, Fred Fairly, his first assistant after all these years and, in a sense, his last throw, must on no account be asked to suffer. Some way must be devised so that Fairly would be able to continue at St Angelicus, unembarrassed and undistressed for the rest of his natural life.

'You won't take anything before you go?'

Fred had forgotten that he had had nothing, on this day of disillusionment and loss, except a cup of tea and two biscuits. 'No thank you, Professor.'

'You will miss Hall, I'm afraid.'

'All the same, no, thank you.'

'Well, I shall see you, then. If you find I have dozed off, which is quite possible, what will you do?'

'I shall worry about that when the time comes,' said Fred, 'I might wake you by playing something on your piano.'

'Oh, but gently, gently.'

The professor looked at him more attentively. 'Yes, you don't look well, that was what you said when you first came in, wasn't it? Are you in any money trouble?'

'I'm unhappy, Professor.'

'Well, perhaps there is no need to wait for the questions. Come straight back.'

*

When Daisy left the hospital at last she asked if she might see Dr Sage. No, he was occupied with a patient, or rather, with several of them. It was a kind of lecture; the patients lectured the doctor, all night if necessary.

'It doesn't matter,' she said. 'I'll write. I'll write him a letter.'

It was a relief of a kind, because she hated leaving Dr Sage. In London he had dosed the patients recklessly, here in Cambridge he seemed less sane than they were, but he brought with him unmistakably the promise of care and trust. He was, too, the very last link she had with the Blackfriars, where she also had once been trusted. Tomorrow, when he read the *Cambridge Evening News*, he would know exactly what she had done, and there would be no trouble finding another girl to do the heavy ironing.

She rode her borrowed bicycle as far as the Wrayburns' house. Mr Wrayburn was out. Mrs Wrayburn was sitting in front of a small fire, relaxing in the knowledge of his being out. Daisy had been trained never to stand at a door letting in draughts, so she went in and shut it behind her, standing against it to show she was on the point of going.

'Goodbye, Mrs Wrayburn. I can't stay in Cambridge any longer, not after what happened in court.'

'No, Daisy, I'm afraid you can't.'

'I didn't expect things to turn out like they have.'

'I'm quite sure you didn't.'

'Who'd have thought of Kelly turning up like that?'

'Who indeed?'

Daisy sighed. 'I've put the cycle and the doorkey where they're supposed to be. I wanted to give you something, though, as a sort of memento.'

'Oh, I don't think I'm likely to forget you, Daisy.' But Daisy persevered, taking the gold ring off her left hand.

'It's got looser since I've been here.'

'No it hasn't, Daisy. It's exactly the same size. You're personifying. A weakness of the English language. You mean that you've got thinner. But in any case, you mustn't give me this. It's a wedding ring.'

'I don't think it is, Mrs Wrayburn. It was my aunt Ellie's, and she never married.'

Mrs Wrayburn had the grace to accept the ring. She felt exhausted. It surprised her to find that Daisy should have had an aunt.

Daisy fetched her few things from the attic. Her box was still at the left luggage at Liverpool Street, never yet sent for. All this time she had relied on her bag, of which, like most wanderers, she had become unreasonably fond. Hairbrush, comb, stays, lavender water, pocket handkerchiefs, prayer book, faithful companions, all of them, back into the bag again. It was a 'Jemima', with expandable elastic sides, but, even so, it gaped.

Out in the road, carrying the overfull Jemima, she felt she looked like someone taking kittens out to drown and changing her mind at the last moment. The rain threatened to get worse. At one point she had had a good, strong umbrella, but not now. She had lent it to one of the two cooks at Dr Sage's, and she hated asking for anything back. It took all the good out of it.

She crossed the road and stood by the ditch, waiting for a lift. As a child she had always dreamed of travelling, but by that she hadn't meant spending half her time between the outskirts of Cambridge and Liverpool Street. Now, at last, with the thought of the sulphur-reeking station and its dark blue ranks of tin placards, her tears came. For hour after hour she had been waiting for a good cry, like a drunkard outside the door of the Jug-and-Bottle. She had thrown away everything. She was deadly frightened that when she got to London Kelly would find her. But she was crying not from fear, but on account of the hurt she had done to Fred.

From here she could see the light in the Wrayburns' front room opposite – one light only until Mr Wrayburn got back, but at the Turners' farm, well set back from the road, every window seemed to blaze, as though they were all keeping it up for some kind of celebration. There were two or three loud shouts from the house and then a creaking and splashing. As a dream repeats itself, Daisy saw a horse and cart coming out of the Turners' entrance. It might have been the same cart, only it was well-lit now with safety oil lamps. It crossed the road, turned right and pulled up where Daisy stood.

There was a woman driving, wrapped up like a parcel in rugs and tarpaulin. She said nothing, so Daisy picked up her bag, wiped her face with the back of her hand, put her foot on the slippery iron pedal, sprang up and edged into the passenger seat. As the cart rocked a little and steadied, the woman said without apparent feeling of any kind, 'I'm going to my sister's at Chesterton. I can't stand any more of that old Turner tonight.'

The horse was evidently unwilling to leave its home as darkness fell. The woman beat it vigorously and it shook its head, throwing off showers of raindrops that glittered in the light of the new headlamp, then started off at a jog trot. It was a slow journey – everything on the road passed them – but not a quiet one. The cart, like a ship at sea, had a pitch as well as a roll, and there was a recurrent screech from a loose spoke on the wheel, along with the creak of the collar and traces and the blowing and rumbling like a deep inner protestation from the horse itself as its feet clocked and clapped in hollow succession on and on. The ride seemed neither short nor long. It was isolated from everyone and everything else on the road by its peaceful, noisy, familiar, monotonous discomfort.

Daisy knew by the lamps that they must have got to the Chesterton Road, where she hoped to catch a motorbus to the station. She had been rocked almost to sleep, but now she turned to the rugs and tarpaulin beside her.

'If you'd be kind enough to slow up, I can jump down. It was very good of you to stop for me. I don't know what I'd have done otherwise.'

'You looked as if you'd lost something, that's why I stopped for you.'

Daisy hesitated. 'You don't know who I am.'

'Yes, I do,' said Mrs Turner.

As the cart's rear light drew away, still at the same slow pace, Daisy stood at the bus-stop in Chesterton Lane, with her back to the wind from the Fens, which was beginning to blow more strongly now, like the tip, but not quite the edge, of a knife. The rain had stopped. Nothing came, not the city motor-bus, nor the bus from the Bull Hotel, which circulated once every hour. Daisy took her nurse's watch out of her coat pocket. It was well past eight. They must have stopped running. She had missed the last one. She set out to walk to the station, and now there was nothing for her to think about except the shortest way through Cambridge to Station Road. Self-reproach, as its habit is, had been waiting patiently for her mind to clear and now it took its opportunity to make, at every point, its blind entrance.

She crossed the river and turned left down Jesus Lane. That was a mistake, she would have to go right again somewhere to get back to St Andrew's Street. Certainly, she ought not to be going down a dimly lit path running along the foot of an ancient stone wall. It was somewhere she had never been before. Too small for a college, perhaps a prison.

Like all the kept-out, she was looking, quite unthinkingly, for a way in. In a few more yards she came to a door as narrow as a good-sized crack, standing wide open. She felt no surprise, although you'd have expected a place like that to lock up as soon as it got dark. She was one of the few people, however, in Cambridge, who would not have been surprised.

All of them would have looked in. She could see a vaulted passageway, not much wider than the gateway, and beyond it green grass and the branches of a tree. Faint light came from the roof of the passageway and from somewhere behind the tree. She now realised that it must, after all, be a college, but she had never been into any of the colleges and had no intention of going into this one.

She heard a very faint cry, a human cry of distress. Without thinking twice about it she walked straight in by the passageway and found an elderly man in black clothes and a gown sitting propped against the trunk of a large tree with gently moving leaves. Daisy knelt down beside him, putting her damp bag down on the grass. He was not drunk, but, poor soul, he was blind. Pulse slow, cold sweat, but nothing worse than that. An ordinary syncope. She put her arms strongly round him and without dragging him, she lowered him, as if it was an easy thing to do, onto the ground. Almost as soon as his head came down to a level with his heart, he stirred and spoke.

'The door!'

Daisy guessed that he had felt the unexpected current of fresh air coming in through the opening. Sometimes very small things can lower the blood pressure in the arteries of the brain. She took his hand.

'There's nothing to worry about.'

Men, also in gowns, were coming out of the lighted chapel opposite. Unfortunately they didn't seem the practical type. At the sight of Daisy they were crying out in dismay and one of them in what sounded like animal terror.

'Now then, this won't help,' she said briskly. 'Don't move him yet. Give nothing by the mouth. Cover him up warm and call the doctor.'

She got up, brushing down her skirt. The patient did not want to let go of her hand, but Daisy was used to this, and gently detached it. In a weak, clear voice he said, 'Surely it can't be . . . ?'

Daisy picked up her bag and leaving the consternation behind her went out the way she had come in, pulling the tall door shut. This was much easier than you would have thought. The iron deadlock clashed tightly home.

She must have spent five minutes in there, not much more. The slight delay, however, meant that she met Fred Fairly walking slowly back to St Angelicus.